Friends Forever

Other Books by Miriam Chaikin about Molly

I SHOULD WORRY, I SHOULD CARE

FINDERS WEEPERS

GETTING EVEN

LOWER! HIGHER! YOU'RE A LIAR!

Friends Forever

by Miriam Chaikin

Drawings by Richard Egielski

HARPER & ROW, PUBLISHERS
Cambridge, Philadelphia, San Francisco, St. Louis, London, Singapore, Sydney
NEW YORK

In memory of my parents, and the aunts—

Friends Forever
Text copyright © 1988 by Miriam Chaikin
Illustrations copyright © 1988 by Richard Egielski
All rights reserved. No part of this book may be
used or reproduced in any manner whatsoever without
written permission except in the case of brief quotations
embodied in critical articles and reviews. Printed in
the United States of America. For information address
Harper & Row Junior Books, 10 East 53rd Street,
New York, N.Y. 10022. Published simultaneously in
Canada by Fitzhenry & Whiteside Limited, Toronto.
10 9 8 7 6 5 4 3 2 1
First Edition

Library of Congress Cataloging-in-Publication Data
Chaikin, Miriam.
    Friends forever.

    "A Charlotte Zolotow book."
    Summary: As news of German victories on
the battlefields and Nazi atrocities against
the Jews comes over the radio, Molly faces
important decisions as she and her Brooklyn
friends prepare to enter junior high school.
    [1. Friendship—Fiction.   2. Jews—United
States—Fiction.   3. Brooklyn (New York, N.Y.)
—Fiction]   I. Egielski, Richard, ill.
II. Title.
PZ7.C3487Fr 1988   [Fic]   86-45777
ISBN 0-06-021203-9
ISBN 0-06-021204-7 (lib. bdg.)

Contents

Friends Forever

1 *Getting Older*

Molly couldn't fall asleep. She told herself the cold was keeping her awake. She pulled the blanket up under her chin and glanced over at the lump in the bed beside her, hoping she hadn't wakened Rebecca, her little sister. She hadn't. The lump was still.

"Brrr," Molly said under her breath, imitating the characters in the comic strips. The apartment never used to be so cold before the war, but now fuel was rationed. Everyone talked about the fuel shortage. Tsippi, her best friend, used to go driving often with her father and stepmother. Not anymore. Not since World War II started, and the rationing began. Her father had enough gas to drive only one day a week, on Sundays.

Molly had been home from school for a week. They had closed down P.S. 164, where she went, to save fuel. That was another thing that was keeping her awake, excitement over the thought of going back to school in the morning. She loved school. She even loved doing homework. And she loved Miss Smith and had missed her.

The secret she had overheard embarrassed her again. Last week, before school closed, Miss Smith had given Molly a note to take to Miss Wissoff, in the teachers' room. Molly had handed over the note. And as she turned to go she heard Miss Wissoff say to another teacher, "Edna's beau is home on furlough. She's getting married over the weekend." Edna—that was Miss Smith. Molly knew the teacher had a boyfriend. The whole class knew it. Molly and Tsippi often wondered together what the boyfriend looked like, what color his eyes were, and his hair. Molly frowned. She had heard stories about things people did when they got married. She did not like to think of Miss Smith that way. The thought made her uncomfortable. It raised questions about her own mother and father. She chased it from her mind.

The mattress dipped and Molly found herself rolling into the dip and feeling the cold as Rebecca shifted and took the blanket with her. Shivering, Molly grabbed back her part of the blanket and flung it over herself. So as not to have to expose her arms to the cold, she kept them under the blanket and, using only her body, wriggled about until she had herself tucked in on all sides.

Molly's thoughts returned to a school worry. She was in the 6B, the graduation class. In the fall, she would go to Montauk, the junior high school. She was sure she would graduate. Her marks were good. But she wanted more than just to graduate. Tsippi was good in all subjects. She had a high average and was going into the RA—the rapid advancement class. That way, she would finish junior high a year early. Some of Molly's other friends were also certain to make the RA. Molly wanted to make it too. But she was afraid her average would not be high enough. That's what worried her. She was terrible in arithmetic. She had to count on her fingers. Sometimes she passed a test, sometimes she failed. It pulled her average down.

Molly shook her head at the darkness. That was only one part of it. What was really worrying her was the arithmetic test coming up in the morning. For the first time in her life, she had decided— She did not want to think about it. She forced her thoughts to the afternoon, to the time after school, when she and her friends were going to pick up the club sweaters they had ordered. She, Tsippi, Little Naomi, and Big Naomi were old friends. Lila and Lily had become friends more recently. All were in the 6B. They were all members of the Borough Park Girls Club. They had saved up from their allowances to buy club sweaters.

The storekeeper had given them only two samples of wool to choose from, both green. "There's a war on," he kept saying. "You can't get whatever color you want." Molly and the girls had chosen the darker green. It was cheaper. And he said he could get it from the factory right away. Molly pictured the sweaters with excitement. They buttoned down the front and had a pocket near the bottom, and on the pocket was a separate circle with the club initials, BPGC. The initial letters were yellow but the man kept calling them gold.

Under the blanket, Molly crossed her fingers, hoping the sweaters really would be ready tomorrow. She and the girls had already gone twice to get them, only to be told that they hadn't come from the factory yet.

Rebecca turned in her sleep again. Molly wriggled to adjust the blanket once more and let her gaze travel across the dark room. She squinted, trying to see how much she could see in the darkness. She was able to make out the two windows on either side of the room. The one on the right Molly thought of as God's window. She treated it with respect because she spoke to God from there. She could almost make out the shape of the brown-painted dresser that stood between the windows. She could not make out the mirror over it, but she knew it was there.

Steering her thoughts, trying to keep them away from the morning, Molly told herself that she ought to start looking in the mirror more often. Not just to practice putting on lipstick, as she sometimes did. And not just to try out new parts in her hair. She was in the 6B and had to start looking nicer. She didn't always remember to comb her hair. And, she didn't know how, but somehow she always had a pencil or ink mark on her lip or cheek.

The thought of the test would not stay away. It stood

up in her mind, forcing her attention on it. She made a face at the darkness. She had decided to cheat on the test. She didn't like the idea. It was a shameful thing to do. But she was afraid not to. If she failed this term's arithmetic tests, she didn't see how she could get into the RA.

A soft moan came from the next room and Molly glanced at the open door. That room was the living room by day. The couch opened up into a bed, and Mama and Papa slept there at night. Yaaki, Molly's little brother, slept there too, in his crib. Molly had heard Mama moan before. The German Nazis were arresting Jews in Europe and killing them. Mama had relations in Europe. She often moaned in her sleep.

Molly heard Yaaki ask for a drink of water, heard Papa get out of bed and head for the kitchen. In that part of the house, off the kitchen, Joey was asleep in his room, the only one in the family with a room of his own.

Turning on her side, finding a new position, Molly wished she could fall asleep. She listened to the sound of Papa's slippers brushing the linoleum floor as he returned with water for Yaaki. She heard the couch creak as Papa got into bed.

All was still in the house but Molly was wide awake. Her thoughts bounced around her fears—of failing, cheating, getting caught. She felt agitated and troubled. She remembered reading about the demons of the night who did not let people fall asleep. Papa had told her, when she spoke of them, that the demons flee when a person says the *Shema* prayer. Molly thought she would try it. She raised her head from the pillow, as a mark of respect, and said softly into the darkness, "*Shema Israel, Adonai Elohenu, Adonai Echad.*" (Hear, O Israel, the Lord is our God, the Lord alone.)

It seemed to Molly after a while that her thoughts had slowed down. Perhaps the demons were leaving. Her eyelids felt like lead. Mama moaned again and called out some words. Molly heard Papa say, "Shhh, shhh." Molly's heart broke, for Mama and her relatives and for all the Jews of Europe. She wished the Messiah, or somebody, would come to help.

Molly wanted to help, to do something. She had already said her nightly prayers. But, feeling sorry for Mama, she got out of bed and stood before God's window for a second time that night. Shivering, hugging herself in her flannel pajamas, her bare feet feeling the cold of the floor, she said, "Please, God, do something to save the Jews from Hitler. And please help the American soldiers and sailors and let the war be over soon."

Shivering, she turned to go. "And let America win," she added, to make clear whose side she was on. She hurried back to bed. "Help the Marines too," she said as she pulled the blanket over her head, realizing she had left them out.

Chilled, moving closer to Rebecca for body warmth but careful not to wake her little sister, Molly closed her eyes. Soon the trembling was gone and she was warm again. She felt heavy and quiet. Gently, she turned over on her side. To her surprise, Eli, a boy in her class, appeared in her thoughts. She wondered what he was doing in her mind. A moment later she fell asleep.

2 *Edna Smith*

In the morning, Molly put on her good-luck dress, a dusty-pink skirt and white top with long sleeves and fake dusty-pink suspenders. The dress was a hand-me-down from the rich cousins. It was snug when it reached her, over a year ago. Now it was too short and too tight. But it was her good-luck dress and she would not think of taking a test without it, especially not an arithmetic test. Books in hand, she went into the kitchen. Papa had already left for work. Everyone else was at the breakfast table.

"You're wearing that dress?" Mama said, inspecting her.

Molly didn't answer as she put her books on the counter and sat down. Mama had been trying for some time to get her to stop wearing that dress.

"It's too small for you," Mama said.

"I don't care," Molly said. She took the cup of cocoa Mama handed her. "It brings me good luck on a test."

"A dress can't help, jerk," Joey said. "You need brains."

Molly looked at her brother. He was already in Montauk Junior High. His best subject was math. She wondered how two members of the same family could be so different.

"Ma," she said, buttering a roll for herself. "Are you sure they didn't make a mistake in the hospital, when they gave you the baby?"

"What baby?" Mama asked.

"Joey," Molly said. "Did they give you the right baby? How can he be so good in arithmetic when I'm so rotten?"

"Just a natural genius," Joey said. "Besides, maybe you were the wrong baby. Did you ever think of that?"

"All of you were the right babies," Mama said, pinching off a piece of her roll and giving it to Yaaki, in the high chair next to her, to eat. "Anyhow," she added, "you'll do your most—and you'll succeed."

"My *best*, Ma," Molly said, correcting her mother.

"You're a good speller, and you get good marks in the other subjects, Molly," Rebecca said.

Molly appreciated the words of comfort from her little sister. "Thank you," she said. She looked down at her good-luck dress. The hand-me-downs from the rich cousins went from Molly to Rebecca. "When this term is over, this dress will be yours," she added.

"What about good luck for a test when you go to Montauk?" Rebecca asked.

Molly hadn't thought about that. "Ha!" she said, not knowing what else to say.

The front door opened and Tsippi came in, bringing in a blast of cold air from the outside. She was wrapped up in a hat and coat and her glasses were steamed up. Tsippi lived a block away, opposite the school. Yet she walked the extra block to Molly's house so they could go to school together.

"Is it cold out?" Mama asked Tsippi.

"Not too," Tsippi said, taking off her glasses and wiping the steam off with her mittens.

"So long," Joey called, rushing out the door.

Hurrying to finish, taking quick sips from her cup, Molly pointed to the chair Joey had vacated, telling Tsippi to sit.

"I'll stand," Tsippi said, going up to Yaaki and fingering his curls. "Why couldn't I have blond curls and blue eyes?" she said.

"What's so hot about blue eyes?" Rebecca asked.

"Brown eyes are beautiful too," Mama said, wiping a crumb from Rebecca's chin.

"Sure they are," Tsippi said, seeming to realize her mistake. "I have brown eyes too. See?" she added, bringing her face close to Rebecca. "You have beautiful brown eyes, and he has beautiful blue eyes," she said.

Molly got up from the table. "I'll be right out," she said, taking her arithmetic book and going toward the bathroom.

"She's so nervous about the test, she's taking the book in there to study," she heard Mama say as she closed the bathroom door.

Molly did not take the book to study. She opened it to the multiplication table and copied out on the palm of her left hand, in ink, the parts she couldn't remember, and also an example of multiplying double numbers, to remind her how to add up the answer. Worry welled up in her as she blew on her hand to dry the ink. She felt like a criminal.

"Come on, Molly," Rebecca said with a knock on the door.

Molly opened the door and went out, careful to keep her left palm toward herself. She intended to show her hand to Tsippi later, when they were alone. That might make her feel less like a criminal, she thought. She put on her coat and took her books. "Okay, let's go," she said.

"Wait a minute. I have to go to the bathroom too," Rebecca said.

The girls left the house to go to school. Molly put her left hand in her pocket and practiced being careful. It was very cold out and she was shivering. "Winter can kill a person," she said, "between the chapped everything and the bleeding. I don't understand how anyone gets to live to be thirteen years old."

"You're almost twelve, and you're still alive," Tsippi said.

"Yeah—but I'm not thirteen, am I?" Molly said.

"You better live," Tsippi said. "I don't want to go to Montauk alone. I don't know anyone there."

The girls stopped at the corner for the traffic light.

Molly made sure her hand was open in her pocket, to keep the writing intact. She wondered if Miss Smith would be in class today. She wanted to talk to Tsippi about the teacher, but not in front of Rebecca. Sometimes, when Molly and her friends didn't want others to understand what they were saying, they spoke the G-language. Molly spoke it now.

"D-gou y-gou th-gink M-giss Sm-gith w-gill c-gome t-go sch-gool t-go d-gay?" (Do you think Miss Smith will come to school today?) she asked.

"Stop it. I don't like it when you do that," Rebecca said. "Talk English!"

"It's private between me and Tsippi," Molly said. "You're too young to hear everything."

"So why don't you wait till I'm not here?" Rebecca said. "Talk about it when you wear your green sweater."

Molly was surprised, as she and the girls crossed, to see that Rebecca was still angry about the sweater. Rebecca had wanted one too. Again and again Mama and Molly had explained that the sweater was for older girls, that they belonged to the same club.

"We'll see when we get there," Tsippi said, answering Molly in English.

"See what?" Rebecca asked.

"If the teacher is here," Tsippi said.

"Is that what the G-language was about?" Rebecca asked.

Tsippi nodded.

14

"What kind of secret is that?" Rebecca said, looking daggers at Molly.

Rebecca turned to go to her class, on the main floor, and Molly and Tsippi went up the stairs. Molly glanced back to make sure she and Tsippi were alone.

"Look," she said, taking her hand out of her pocket and showing the writing to Tsippi.

"Molly!" Tsippi said, looking surprised.

"Tsippi," Molly said. "You know how rotten I am. If I don't pass, I won't make the RA."

"What if you get caught?" Tsippi said.

Molly's stomach flipped. "I won't," she said, trying to sound more cheerful than she felt.

"What if Beverly notices?" Tsippi said.

Beverly, Molly's seatmate, was the school trouble-maker. Nobody liked her. Molly never spoke to her if she didn't have to.

"I'll be careful," she said, and put her hand back inside her pocket. She thought about Beverly with disgust. "The best thing about graduating is I won't have to sit next to her anymore, in a new school," she added.

"You hope," Tsippi said.

The girls arrived at the classroom door and glanced inside.

"She's here," Molly said. "I'm embarrassed to look at her."

"You mean about the wedding?" Tsippi said.

Molly nodded.

16

"Me too," Tsippi said.

"Did you forget how to go inside?" a voice asked behind them.

Molly turned and saw Eli. As she stepped aside to let him pass she was again surprised that he had been in her thoughts the night before.

"Wish me luck," she said to Tsippi.

"Good luck—and watch out," Tsippi said, pointing her chin toward Beverly, Molly's seatmate, in the first row.

Molly didn't feel her usual self as she hung up her coat in the wardrobe. Her hand was shaking. It wasn't only that she was nervous about getting caught. Confessing to Tsippi hadn't helped. Now, in the daylight, standing in the same room with the teacher, she felt shame.

Eyes straight ahead, Molly hurried to her seat. Already, Beverly was squirming, looking about, watching who knew what. Molly always ignored her. Today, she had to ignore her double. She slid into her seat without a word.

Careful to keep her hand from Beverly's gaze, Molly arranged her books in her desk. Much as she wanted to look fully at the teacher, all she could do was steal glances at her.

Miss Wissoff came in to speak to Miss Smith. Molly, resting her hand in her lap, now allowed herself to look directly at the teacher. She wore a plaid skirt and brown sweater set that Molly had seen before. The only difference was the wedding ring, which Molly noticed with embarrassment.

Miss Wissoff left as the starting bell rang, and Miss Smith closed the door and came to the front of the class.

"Good morning," she said.

"Good morning," Molly answered with the others, almost forgetting about her hand and starting to bring it up.

"I have some news," Miss Smith said.

Molly's heart raced. Was she going to tell about the wedding?

"Mr. Brooke, our principal, has joined the Army," Miss Smith said.

Molly was disappointed.

"Also," Miss Smith said, "I was going over the cards this morning and I noticed that not all of you have chosen a foreign language to study in junior high."

"If we don't graduate, we don't have to worry about taking a foreign language," a voice called.

"If a foreign language worries you, I can fix it so you get left back," Miss Smith said.

Molly smiled, then winced at the sound of Beverly's raucous laugh.

Miss Smith nodded toward the back.

"Yes, Eli?" she said.

Molly had never really paid attention to Eli before. He sat in back, on Beverly's side of the room. Palm facedown in her lap, she swung around in her seat toward the aisle, to avoid having to meet Beverly's eyes, to look at him. Eli had dirty-blond hair, brown eyes, and a dimple in his chin. Tsippi had once said that some girls thought he was the handsomest boy in the class.

"I was thinking of taking Latin," Eli said. "But everybody says it's a dead language. I don't know what to do."

Molly faced front as the teacher began to speak.

"It's true that Latin, the language of the ancient Romans, is not spoken today," Miss Smith said. "But it is far from dead. If you know Latin, you will more easily learn French, Spanish, and Italian. What's more, Latin is the language of science. Trees and flowers have Latin names."

She took a piece of chalk. "The Latin name of sunflower is *helianthus*," she said, writing the Latin on the board. "The botanist in Norway doesn't know the word sunflower. Neither does the French botanist. But all botanists everywhere know the Latin name, *helianthus*. Latin is their common language."

Molly had long ago decided to take French. She had never heard anyone speak Latin in movies or in books. Besides, she had expected to go to work when she graduated from high school, so she could help the family with money. That was why she had signed up for a commercial course. French came with it.

Miss Smith took an eraser and cleared the board. "And now for the moment you have all been waiting for," she said, facing the class.

Groans and grunts came from around the room.

Miss Smith removed a stack of printed tests from her drawer and gave a batch to the first person in each row. Molly, nervousness growing, held her left hand toward herself as she took a copy of the test and passed the others back.

"Be sure to write your names at the top—in ink," Miss Smith said.

Molly saw Beverly writing away. Molly framed the test with her left arm, as if to hide it from Beverly. Beverly copied during spelling, history, and geography tests, but not during arithmetic. She was good at it. Even so, Molly maintained her arm in that position. She flicked up her palm to see if the writing was still there. Then she dipped her pen into the inkwell, wrote her name at the top of the page, and glanced at the first two examples:

- A wholesaler filled 5,750 Halloween packages with 1,100 candy corns in each package. How many candy corns were used in all?

- A gasoline truck carries 5,998 gallons of gasoline. If the truck made 1,275 trips in a year, how many gallons of gasoline did it carry during the year?

The questions made her sick. Her hand was sweating, and she had to raise it up a little to let the air dry it. Feeling small, and careful about her hand, Molly tackled the easy problems first, then did the next-hard ones with some help from her hand, and skipped altogether the really hard ones. When she finished she got up and brought her test to Miss Smith and asked for permission to leave the room.

Molly hurried across the hall to the girls' bathroom and washed the writing from her hand. She looked at the clean hand, feeling relieved. It wasn't easy to cheat, she thought. Molly glanced at herself in the mirror, to see if she looked the same. She took a deep breath, and returned to class. She realized, as she took her seat and looked at the teacher, that the pressures of the morning had washed away her embarrassment over the fact that Miss Smith was now a married lady.

3 Aunt Bessie Moves In

On Thursday, Molly sat in class on pins and needles, waiting—and dreading—to hear the results of the test. Miss Smith had said she would give them out today. But the morning passed without a word from the teacher. At last, after lunch, she removed the tests from her desk drawer. Holding them close to her chest, she came around to the front of the desk and said slowly, "Two people have failed—"

Molly's heart sank.

"But they're not in our class," the teacher added, smiling and giving out the tests.

Molly could hardly believe her ears. That meant she had passed! Bursting with joy, she turned to share her pleasure with Tsippi. Molly took the sheet Miss Smith handed her and looked at it. There were red crosses for wrong answers, but they hardly mattered. The P for passing was what counted. Molly glanced over and saw that Beverly had received a B. She didn't care. Beverly could have received a triple A. Molly had passed. That was all that mattered.

The good news seemed to Molly to be an omen for a good day. The girls were meeting to go for their sweaters again after school (the sweaters hadn't been ready again on Monday), and Molly was sure they would be ready on this good-luck day. She wrote a note to Tsippi, saying: *The sweaters will be ready—I can feel it in my bones*, and slipped it to the girl behind to pass back.

When all the tests had been given out, Miss Smith seated herself on Molly's desk. Thrilled to be favored in that way, Molly's heart skipped a beat. The teacher began speaking about the products being rationed—shoes, coffee, sugar, lentils, raisins, and other things.

"Everyone feels the pinch of war," Miss Smith said. "The shortages are not pleasant. But they are nothing compared to the dangers and hardships faced by our servicemen."

Molly thought about Miss Smith's boyfriend, now husband.

"Yes, Fortunata?" Miss Smith said, nodding toward the back of the room.

Molly decided to turn and look at Fortunata so she could steal a glance at Eli. Since Miss Smith sat on the aisle side of Molly's desk, Molly turned in her seat the other way and was offended to find herself gazing into Beverly's eyes. Molly hurriedly removed her glance, looked at Eli, saw Tsippi answer her note by holding up crossed fingers to say, "I wish," and turned her attention to Fortunata.

"It's funny, Miss Smith," Fortunata was saying. "They made a new ration, only three pairs of shoes a year?"

Miss Smith nodded.

"Me and my sisters and brothers—all we ever get is one pair of shoes a year—for Easter. What kind of ration is that?"

Molly laughed. The same was true in her family. "We get only one pair of shoes too," she said. "For Passover."

"The rich people can afford to throw out their shoes and buy new ones," somebody called.

The children began to talk all at once.

"Boys and girls!" Miss Smith said, asking for silence.

Molly stole another glance at Eli, then, closing her eyes to avoid seeing Beverly's face, faced front.

Miss Smith stood up. "That's true," she said, walking away. "The rations do not represent a hardship for some people."

Molly remembered a poem she liked and raised her hand, wanting to tell it.

"We poor people have to wear the same shoes for a whole year," she said. "For us it's like the poem says: 'Use it up, wear it out, make it do, or do without.' "

"Right!" Fortunata called from the back.

Geography was next, and Miss Smith went to the

board and pulled down the wall map. She took up a pointer.

"The war, at last, is turning in our favor," she said. She named and pointed to the countries that Germany had so far conquered. "Austria, Czechoslovakia, Poland, Denmark, Norway, Holland, Belgium, France. The fighting is now going on here," she said, moving the pointer to Russia. "Our Russian allies have stopped the Germans," she added with a pleased expression, "and are driving them back."

Molly could hardly wait for the afternoon to be over. She kept glancing up at the wall clock. When, at last, the three o'clock bell rang, she and Tsippi hurried to the wardrobe for their coats and ran downstairs to the main entrance, to meet their friends.

One by one, the girls, all members of the club, all in the 6B, arrived from their own classes. The cousins, Big and Little Naomi, were all excited about the sweaters.

A moment later, Lila and Lily came hurrying over.

"Boy-oh-boy," Lila said, rubbing her wool mittens together in anticipation.

"Listen to her," Lily said with a smile, just as excited.

"What are we waiting for? Let's go," Lila said.

"We have to wait for my little sister," Molly said. "I have to bring her home. We pass right by the house," she added.

Rebecca soon appeared in a sea of children crowding the hallway, hat in hand and her jacket unzipped. Molly pulled up the zipper and tied the hat on. Then she and the girls walked Rebecca home and walked on down to Thirteenth Avenue.

"I'll kill myself if the sweaters aren't ready again," Little Naomi said.

"Why kill yourself?" Big Naomi said. "Kill the man."

When the girls entered the store, the man was standing behind the counter, smoking a cigar. Molly could tell from the expression on his face that the sweaters weren't there. He took the cigar from his mouth.

"They didn't come yet," he said.

"You told us to come back today," Molly said.

"I said 'maybe,' " he said and looked away. "There's a—" he began. He always said the same thing. Molly and the girls knew how the sentence ended and finished it with him. "—war on."

He took an envelope from a shelf behind him. "These came in, though," he said, shaking the club emblems out onto the counter. Excited, Molly and the girls huddled over the counter, touching and exclaiming over the circular cloth patches with the club letters BPGC set in the middle.

"When the sweaters come in, we'll sew those on the pockets, one-two-three, and you'll have your sweaters," the man said. "Try again next week. Only—" he added, looking from girl to girl, "why do all of you have to come? Can't just one or two of you come?"

"It's all our sweaters," Tsippi said, indicating the girls with her glance.

26

"There's no room in the store for customers, if you all come," the man said, and shoved his cigar back into his mouth.

"What are we?" Molly said, indignant.

Disappointed, she and the girls left and stood outside propping each other up with comforting words.

"Actually, it's too cold to wear a sweater," Molly said, trying to put a good face on things.

"That's true," Lila said.

"A club sweater is supposed to be seen," Lily said. "We'd have to wear it under the coat, in this weather."

"It'll never fit under a coat, it's too bulky," Lila said.

Big Naomi looked up. "There's Julie," she said. "Julie!" she called.

Julie had frizzy red hair that she was always blowing out of her eyes. Waving a small package that she held, she came running. Molly recognized the package, delicatessen wrapping paper, and wondered if Julie's mother ever gave her anything besides baloney to eat.

Molly felt sorry for Julie. Julie's father had run away with another woman. Ever since, her mother never left the house and never did anything. She made Julie iron and wash dishes and even made her stay home to play cards with her. And she wouldn't give Julie money to buy a sweater. Molly and her friends thought Julie's mother was selfish.

"D-gon't s-gay g-any-th-ging ga-b'gout th-ge sw-ge-t-ger," Molly said.

"Hi!" she and the girls said.

"Hi!" Julie answered, blowing the hair out of her eyes. She noticed they were standing in front of the sweater store. "Did you get your sweaters yet?" she asked.

"Not yet," Tsippi said.

Molly was surprised that Julie knew about the sweaters. "It's wartime, the man keeps saying," she said. "Come on, walk with us," she added.

The girls walked down the avenue together. A different girl dropped away at each corner to go home. Molly and Tsippi said good-bye to Julie and walked on alone to Forty-third Street, where they both lived.

"I feel sorry for her," Molly said. "Lila's mother is strict, but she's fair. Not like Julie's mother."

"Yeah," Tsippi said. "Lila's mother says, 'Be back such-and-such a time.' But at least she lets Lila go. Julie's mother doesn't let her leave the house."

"Like a slave," Molly added.

The girls arrived at Molly's house and paused in front of the stoop.

"I never saw Julie's mother without that men's bathrobe she always wears," Molly said.

"And what about those curlers?" Tsippi said.

Molly looked at Tsippi. "It's funny, though," she said. "Julie doesn't seem to mind. Notice how she's never angry or upset? She's always in a good mood."

"Not like some girls we know," Tsippi said.

Molly wasn't sure which girls Tsippi meant, but she wasn't interested enough to ask. "You want to come in, and we'll do homework together?" she said.

Tsippi shook her head as she pushed her glasses up on her nose. "My stepmother's ladies are coming to roll bandages for the Red Cross. She likes me to be around," she said.

"Then come over later to listen to the radio," Molly said as she went up the steps.

"If I can," Tsippi called over her shoulder, walking off.

Inside, Molly had a surprise. Her aunt Bessie was sitting at the kitchen table with Mama, sipping tea. Aunt Bessie never came during the week. She came on Fridays, to spend *shabbos*—the Sabbath—with Molly's family, then went home to Coney Island, and Heshy, her husband. Aunt Bessie's trunk and suitcase were on the floor. Molly knew in her bones that something was wrong. Heshy was not a nice man. She had heard stories. . . .

"Hi," she said, giving her aunt a kiss.

"Aunt Bessie's coming to live with us again," Mama said.

Molly knew it! Nobody in the family liked Heshy. He was a waiter in a restaurant on the boardwalk.

"I hope Heshy isn't coming here too," Molly said, sensing she was on safe ground and glad to be able to express her opinion about him freely.

"No more Heshy," Mama said, and took a sip of tea. "Aunt Bessie is getting a divorce."

Molly was glad. "I never liked him or his smelly cigar," she said, to show whose side she was on.

"Finished," Aunt Bessie said, looking sad, staring at the window.

"Where's Rebecca? And Yaaki?" Molly asked, to change the subject.

"Yaaki's in the living room," Mama said. "Rebecca's by Mrs. Chiodo. Put your books away and come have milk," she added.

Yaaki was playing with some clothespins in the living room. Molly ruffled his curls as she went by. She thought about her little sister. For a long time Mrs. Chiodo, the lady next door, had been Rebecca's only friend. Rebecca now had a second friend, Shirley, an older girl on the street. Shirley's father had died. Usually the boy in the family went to the synagogue nearly every day for a year, to say *kaddish*, the prayer for the dead. There were no boys in Shirley's family, so she went. Rebecca sometimes went along.

Molly reminded herself to look in the mirror as she put her books on the dresser. She saw that her part was crooked, but she was too lazy to do anything about it.

She glanced around the room she shared with her sister. A folding bed stood folded against the wall. Aunt Bessie would now be sharing the room permanently. That would be her bed.

Molly returned to the kitchen. There were bread and butter and jam on the table, and she took a glass of milk and sat down with her aunt and mother.

"Nu—what happened with the test?" Mama asked.

"I passed," Molly said, feeling awkward.

"You see? You worried for nothing," Mama said.

Molly didn't want her mother to think she had done well.

"I almost didn't," she said, smearing a piece of bread with butter and jam. "I was on the border. I could have failed."

"You could have been a wagon, if you had wheels," Mama said.

Molly bit into the bread, anxious to end the subject. The front door opened and Rebecca came in.

"Where is it?" Rebecca asked, getting out of her coat.

"What?" Molly asked.

"The sweater," Rebecca said.

Molly wished Rebecca would stop thinking about the sweater. "It wasn't ready again," she said. "Isn't it great?" she added in a cheery voice. "Aunt Bessie's coming to live with us again."

Yaaki came in from the living room and climbed up onto Aunt Bessie's lap.

"I know, I gave her my drawer," Rebecca said.

"You had nothing in it but the picture of the little girl with red cheeks, from the soup advertisement," Molly said.

"She'll still be there," Rebecca said.

"That's right," Aunt Bessie said. "I'll take care of the little girl, and use the rest of the drawer."

Molly hoped she wasn't going to be asked to give up any drawer space. "Joey has that whole dresser in his room," she said. "What's in it?"

"Never mind," Mama said. "You don't have to worry. I'll make room."

To cover up a feeling of selfishness Molly decided to tease Aunt Bessie. Her aunt snored, and they all often laughed about it with her.

"Rebecca," Molly said. "Do you think we should make any rules, now that Aunt Bessie will be sleeping with us all the time?"

"What about?" Rebecca said.

"Snoring," Molly said.

Rebecca smiled. Aunt Bessie looked up. "Oh, I'm glad you mentioned it," she said. "Somebody in there snores. I think we should make a rule, *No snoring.*"

Molly laughed with the others. Aunt Bessie used to make jokes before she got married, then she had stopped. Molly hoped her aunt was going to start being funny again now.

Molly did her homework and read in her library book. After a while, everyone was home and the family sat down to supper. Papa hadn't been surprised to find Aunt Bessie there. Molly guessed he had known in advance. Her aunt seemed jollier during supper and more like her old self. After supper, everyone went into the living room to listen to the radio.

Papa sat in the green chair, under the picture of Jabotinsky, the Jewish leader. Molly sat on the couch with Mama and Aunt Bessie, and Rebecca and Yaaki sat on the floor. Joey sat on the arm of the couch. The sound on the radio would not come up unless someone held the loose wire in back. Joey sat there so he could hold the wire.

Major Bowes and His Original Amateur Hour featured a soprano, a comedian, then a boy singing "Comin' In on a Wing and a Prayer."

"Joey," Aunt Bessie said, "you have a better voice. Why don't you go on the radio?"

"Sure, sure," Joey said.

"That's why he's so crazy about you," Molly said to Aunt Bessie. "You keep complimenting him."

The news came on next.

"Let's hope there's good news tonight," Papa said, imitating the voice of Gabriel Heatter, the announcer.

Molly smiled at Papa.

"Joey, as soon as he gives the war news, switch to the Jewish station," Papa said. "They give more Jewish news there."

Gabriel Heatter's voice filled the room.

Ah, there's good news tonight.

Molly glanced at Papa and smiled.

The war has taken a definite turn for the better. The Russian winter is proving a mighty foe for the Germans, and Hitler's troops are being driven back and suffering heavy losses. The Germans are not the supermen they claimed to be.

"Supermen, my foot!" Joey said.

"Shhh," Papa said. "Change the station, Joey," he

33

added as the announcer began to tell about a miners' strike. Joey turned the dial and a new voice filled the room.

—We knew the Nazis were deporting the Jews of the Warsaw Ghetto, but we didn't know until now where. They are being deported to concentration camps. Some say they are being killed there.

"Oy!" Mama cried, as her hand flew to her chest.

The words felt like a punch to Molly's stomach. She couldn't look up, she couldn't stand to see the misery on the faces of her parents and aunt. That night, she stood for a long time before God's window. She thought of telling God that she would never cheat again if God did something to save the Jews, but she couldn't bring herself to do that. Instead she promised to obey her parents, to help others, to do good deeds, to give to charity, and to love her neighbors and maybe even try to be a little more friendly to Beverly—if God helped.

4 The Sweaters Come

The days went by and before Molly knew it, February was over, Purim and St. Patrick's Day had passed, and she and the girls made a final trip to the sweater store and left with sweaters in their hands—at last. They had not yet worn them. They had agreed to wait until Sunday, when they could all put them on at the same time and go out walking.

On Sunday, Molly's kitchen crowded up as, one by one, her friends appeared in sweaters, brimming over with excitement.

"We're so lucky," Molly said. "The first time that we can wear them, and we have a beautiful day."

"This is the part I love best," Tsippi said, stroking the club emblem on the pocket.

Yaaki came out of Joey's room and marched through the kitchen. "There's too much people in here," he said, heading for the living room, where Papa and Aunt Bessie were sitting, reading their papers.

Mama, leaning over the sink and scrubbing clothes on the washboard, looked up. "He's right," she said. "Why don't you go outside? It's crowded in here."

"We're waiting for Lily," Molly said.

"Why can't you wait outside?" Mama asked.

"No," Molly said. "We want to all step out into the street in the same minute."

"Like the rain?" Mama said.

"Like a parade," Molly said.

"Like pickles," Rebecca said, sulking near the window.

Molly glanced at her little sister, wishing she would get over her hurt feelings. When Molly had brought the sweater home, Rebecca's resentment had flared up all over again.

The front door opened and Lily came in, grinning from ear to ear and stroking her green sweater.

"Aren't they beautiful?" Molly said.

"You look like a bunch of grapes," Mama said.

"We're all here now," Little Naomi said. "Let's go."

As Molly and her friends turned to the door, Rebecca's friend, Shirley, the older girl, came in. Shirley gave Mama and Molly a friendly smile. "I'm going to the synagogue to say kaddish," she said to Mama. "Rebecca said yesterday she wanted to go with me."

"Shirley says kaddish for her father," Molly explained to her friends. "Rebecca goes to *shul* with her sometimes," she added, putting pride in her voice so Rebecca would hear the compliment.

Mama wiped her hands on her apron and turned to Rebecca. "Take a sweater, in case it gets chilly," she said.

Molly wished Mama had used some other word. Rebecca felt badly enough without hearing the word sweater again.

"Come on," Lila said, opening the door. "It's hot in here."

"See you later," Molly called over her shoulder as she ran out with her friends.

The girls huddled in the hall for a moment. Molly took the hands of the two closest to her, and the other girls also joined hands.

"Friends forever!" they said together, reciting the club motto.

Then they ran outside and headed for Thirteenth Avenue.

"Everybody's out on such a nice day," Big Naomi said. "The whole world will see us."

"Yeah," Lily laughed.

"Let's walk down to Thirty-ninth Street on one side, and up to Fiftieth on the other," Molly said.

The girls paraded around the neighborhood all afternoon, up and down the avenue and in and out of side streets. When they passed Lila's house they went in for a drink of water, and when they came out, Molly had a surprise. Eli was walking on the other side of the street, wearing knickers, playing a harmonica, and delivering dry cleaning. Molly had never seen him outside of school before. He didn't see her, or anyone. He just walked along, playing to himself.

Molly was surprised by the excitement she felt. She *thought* it was excitement, anyhow. Usually excitement made her loud and jumpy. She felt pleasant and cozy now. Molly decided not to speak of her feeling. She and her friends prided themselves on not being boy crazy, like some of the girls at school.

"It's getting cold," Little Naomi said when they reached the corner.

"I better get home too," Tsippi said, looking up at the sky. "My stepmother's friends are coming to roll bandages."

"My knees are turning blue," Lila said.

"Your knees? Look at my hands," Lily said, showing her hands around.

"Into each life some rain must fall," Big Naomi said as they walked along. "Now I have to go home and study for an arithmetic test."

Molly winced. The cozy, secret feeling she had been enjoying was gone. She had a test in the morning too. "Don't remind me," she said.

The girls walked on, each one falling away from the group at her own corner. Molly and Tsippi left the others and turned up Forty-third Street.

"We're lucky," Molly said. "They're the nicest girls in the whole school."

"And the smartest," Tsippi said.

Up the street Molly saw people gathered in front of her house. She didn't like the look of it.

"My mother and father!" she said, seeing her parents and running.

Mama was biting her knuckles. Papa and some neighbors were trying to calm her.

"What happened?" Molly asked, frightened.

"Rebecca," Mama said. "They kidnapped her."

The words struck terror in Molly's heart.

"Try to calm down," Papa said to Mama. "Nobody kidnapped her."

"Then where is she?" Mama said, clasping and unclasping her hands. "My baby! Somebody kidnapped my child."

The neighbors standing around were all trying to comfort Mama and tell her there was nothing to worry about. "She's not kidnapped. She's fine. You'll see," they said.

Molly noticed Shirley and remembered that Shirley had come to call for Rebecca. "What happened, Shirley?" she asked.

"I brought her home myself," Shirley said. "My mother made poppy-seed cookies, which Rebecca loves." She looked at the paper bag in her hand. "I brought some down for Rebecca—but she wasn't here." She looked at Molly with a worried face. "Your mother never saw her."

"But you said you brought her home," Molly said.

"I brought her here, to the steps," Shirley said, nodding at the stoop.

"Maybe she's at Mrs. Chiodo's," Molly said.

"Mrs. Chiodo's not home," Mama said, clasping and unclasping her hands.

Molly's heart was in a knot. She felt dumb, unable to move, and saw only Tsippi looking at her with sad eyes.

"Molly, I have to go," Tsippi said apologetically.

Even in her distress, Molly was annoyed. She thought a lost child was more important than rolling bandages. "Go ahead," she said.

"She'll be found, I'm sure," Tsippi said, calling over her shoulder as she ran.

"Your brother and aunt are out looking for her now," Shirley said. "They're going from house to house. Nobody kidnapped her," she added. "She's somewhere—"

Molly's heart was beating with fear. But Shirley had to be right. Rebecca had to be somewhere. She was afraid to cross alone. She never went with strangers. She couldn't have gone far. A picture of Rebecca sulking in the kitchen came to Molly's mind.

"The sweater!" she said, taking herself by surprise. "Ma, Pa," she called. "She's still mad about the sweater. She's hiding to get even."

"Where is she getting even?" Mama asked, quieter now.

"I don't know," Molly said, not sure she was right, but hoping she was. "I'll go look for her," she said.

Papa took Mama by the arm. "Come in now. Yaaki's alone in the house. He'll wake up soon. He'll get scared if he sees nobody."

"Yeah, go inside, wait inside," Molly heard a neighbor say as she hurried up the street. She stopped at Shimmy's house, a little boy Rebecca sometimes played with, but Shimmy's mother said Joey had already been there. Molly kept walking, watching both sides of the street, going up each stoop and looking in every hallway. Around the corner she stood on tiptoe to peer over the painted window of the missionary store, although she knew Rebecca was afraid of the place and would not go in there willingly.

Molly walked down the next block, looking and looking. On the wall of the Labor Lyceum she saw a large poster that said, CHANNA DUBROVINSKY AND HER ACTORS—SUNDAY ONLY. Molly went inside.

The lobby was empty, but she could hear actors' voices through the closed door. She opened the door and tiptoed into the darkened auditorium. The audience was watching the actors on the stage. She walked down the center aisle, peering into the faces of the people on both sides.

Someone seized her arm, and she saw a man with a flashlight standing at her side.

"Are you looking for your seat, girlie?" the man said, shining the flashlight on the floor.

"I'm looking for my little sister," Molly said.

"Shhh," the people in the audience hissed.

"If you don't have a seat, you can't stay," the man said.

"Here's a seat, Molly," Rebecca's voice said.

Molly's heart flipped with joy at the sight of her little sister's small form among the adult figures in the next row.

"That's my sister!" Molly said. "Rebecca, come out!"

"Quiet! Shut up!" the audience called. A man jumped up out of his seat. "Get her out of here! And get out of here yourself!" he said to the usher.

"Come with me," the usher said, pulling Molly by the arm.

"Rebecca, come," Molly said, shaking him off. She saw Rebecca leave her seat.

In the lobby, Molly melted with happiness at the sight of her little sister.

"Where were you?" she asked, realizing it was a stupid question.

"Here," Rebecca said.

"Mama's so worried about you," Molly said. "Papa too. The whole neighborhood's looking for you."

"Was the kid lost?" the usher asked.

Molly nodded.

"Why didn't you say so in the first place?" he said.

Molly took Rebecca by the hand and went outside with her. She was filled with happiness as they walked home hand in hand.

"You made everybody worry so," Molly said.

Rebecca was silent.

"Why did you do it, Rebecca?" Molly asked, keeping her voice gentle.

Rebecca said nothing.

"Was it on account of the sweater?" Molly asked.

Rebecca nodded.

Molly felt a stab of remorse. "If I knew it was going to bother you so much, I never would have gotten it," she said. "I love you. I don't love this dumb old sweater," she added. She saw Rebecca wipe away a tear.

"I was scared too," Rebecca said. "I'm glad you found me, Molly."

Molly felt weepy and brushed a tear from her own eye.

"They found Rebecca!" a woman leaning out the window hollered as Molly and Rebecca turned onto Forty-third Street.

"You see, Rebecca," Molly said. "The whole block was worried."

The girls hurried up the steps of the stoop. Inside, there were shrieks of delight and tears and a shower of kisses for Rebecca.

"What made you go in the Labor Lyceum?" Joey asked Molly. "I went right by it."

Molly shrugged. "I didn't know where else to look," she said.

She left the rest of the family in the kitchen to fuss over Rebecca and went into her room and closed the door. She went up to God's window and opened it, so she would be better heard.

"I'm always asking you for favors, God," she said. "It's high time I thanked you. Thanks," she said, as the tears streamed from her eyes.

5 *The Second Test*

Miss Smith finished writing on the board the last part of the division test: "There are 168 hours in one week. How many whole weeks are there in 9,216 hours? How many are left over?"

Sitting in her pink good-luck dress, Molly watched the board. The test looked hard. She placed her left arm around the sheet on her desk, taking care not to let Beverly see her hand. Molly began, doing the easy problems first. To do the first of the harder problems, she lifted her left palm ever so slightly, so she could see the sample she had written there. She thought she saw Beverly lean over to look at her hand. Nervous, Molly flattened her hand on her desk and continued. She did as many examples as she could before the bell rang.

"The ones in back, please collect the tests from your row," Miss Smith said.

Molly handed her test to Eli, hoping he wouldn't notice the blank spaces she had left. When she turned back, she found Beverly almost standing at her seat, leaning over into Molly's. Frightened, Molly gave Beverly a dirty look and dropped her hand in her lap. She didn't know if Beverly was just squirming, or if she was trying to see something. Molly waited a couple of minutes after Miss Smith began the geography lesson, then raised her hand for permission to leave and went out to wash her hand in the girls' bathroom.

She found it hard to concentrate the rest of the morning. Her thoughts whirled. Now she was frightened, now ashamed. She would never make the RA if she were caught cheating. And how disappointed Miss Smith would be. Miss Smith liked her. Tsippi teased Molly sometimes about being the teacher's pet. "And what about my own honor?" Molly thought.

The last class of the morning was carpentry for boys and sewing for girls. When the bell rang, Miss Smith said she had been saving the good news for last and that the class didn't have to come back after lunch.

The children made noises of gladness.

"The teachers have a meeting with the new principal," she said. "But there is homework. I want you to write a composition about I Am an American Day."

"You mean about patriotism and honesty, Miss Smith?" Beverly asked.

Molly wondered if the remark was directed at her.

"Whatever being an American means to you," Miss Smith said. "See you tomorrow."

As the class got up to leave, Molly hung back. She

wanted to see what Beverly did. If Beverly stopped to speak to the teacher, Molly would know Beverly had seen and was telling. Molly pretended to be looking for something inside her desk, but she kept an eye on Beverly and was relieved to see her go directly to the door.

Tsippi came up alongside Molly. "It wasn't too bad, was it?" she asked.

"What?" Molly asked.

"The arithmetic test—"

Molly made a face. She had almost forgotten about that part. "It was hard for me," she said, going from the room with Tsippi.

On the way to the sewing class, Molly told Tsippi of her fears.

"She probably didn't see anything," Tsippi said. "You know how nosy she is. She's a squirmer, and she could have been looking at ten different things."

"You don't think she saw?" Molly said.

"You said you were careful," Tsippi said.

Molly had been careful. But Beverly was quick and sharp.

"It's your imagination," Tsippi said.

"I hope so," Molly said, as they entered Miss Genkin's class.

Miss Genkin, the sewing teacher, was also the gym teacher. She handed each girl a packet, and Molly and Tsippi headed for seats near the door.

"The best thing about sewing is I don't have to sit next to that twerp," Molly said, casting a glance at Beverly on the other side of the room. Molly wanted to believe that she had nothing to worry about. She told herself it *was* her imagination, and took up the sewing things: the tissue-paper pattern, material, a pair of scissors, and a needle and thread.

"What do you think it is?" Molly asked Tsippi, examining the pattern.

Tsippi shrugged. "An apron?"

"Lay the pattern over the material and cut along the dotted line," Miss Genkin said from the side of her mouth. "When you finish cutting, bring it to me, so I can check before you start sewing."

"What is it, Miss Genkin?" someone asked.

"A pillowcase," the teacher said.

Molly glanced at Tsippi and shrugged.

"Which side is up?" someone called.

"The top," Miss Genkin said.

Molly arranged the pattern and material in her lap. She glanced at Beverly and saw her cutting away. Maybe Tsippi was right. Molly took up the scissors and began cutting. When she was through, she brought her work to Miss Genkin. Molly heard laughter as she went to the window, where the teacher was standing so she could see in the good light.

"Molly!" Tsippi called in a loud whisper.

Molly felt the class was laughing at her, but she didn't know why. The class roared as she held up her work for the teacher to inspect.

Miss Genkin smiled out of the corner of her mouth.

"Looks like you cut clear through," she said, gazing down at the skirt of Molly's dress.

Molly looked down. She had cut a square out of the upper half of her skirt! The part that had been cut hung down, and her bloomers showed. Her first worry was for the dress.

"My good-luck dress!" she cried, pulling up the flap to cover herself.

"Better get a rabbit's foot—that dress is finished," Miss Genkin said.

Although Molly was embarrassed and upset, the class laughter was so great, she couldn't help smiling at her predicament.

Miss Genkin gave Molly some light-colored thread.

"Just sew it up good enough to get home," the teacher said.

Molly went back to her seat and, with loose stitches, attached the two pieces together. After class Tsippi walked with Molly to the school yard gate, going in front of her, to hide her. Then Molly walked home alone, holding her books low in front of herself, to cover the sewing.

Mama, Rebecca, and Yaaki were sitting at the kitchen table.

"Look!" she said as she entered, and told them what had happened.

"Show me," Yaaki said, straining to see. Molly went closer to the highchair, to show him.

Mama took the skirt in her fingers and looked at it. "That's how they teach you to sew?" she said.

"It wasn't real sewing," Molly said. "It was just to hold the pieces together, so I could walk in the street."

"You won't be able to wear that dress anymore, thank God," Mama said.

"It was supposed to be my dress next," Rebecca said.

Frightened to let Rebecca become upset about anything after yesterday, Molly said, "You'll have your own good-luck dress, a better one, won't she, Ma?"

"I'll buy you a new dress, just for tests," Mama said.

"Can we afford it?" Rebecca said.

"We're not so poor anymore," Molly said. "We're better off now, since Papa started the defense job, aren't we, Ma?"

Mama nodded. There were peanut butter and jelly sandwiches on the table. She brought the pot of tomato soup from the stove. "Thank God," she said, ladling out soup.

Molly sat down at the table.

"My good-luck dress," she said sadly, as she bit into a sandwich.

"Dress?" Mama said. "Even last year, it was already almost an undershirt."

After lunch, Mama put Yaaki to bed, then Molly, Rebecca, and Mama sat around the kitchen table. Molly and Rebecca did homework. Mama was studying to become a citizen of the United States, and she was reading her book, *The Citizen*.

"Let's see if you know," Mama said. "Who was the first president of the United States?"

Molly let Rebecca answer such an easy question.

"George Washington," Rebecca said. "They have a picture of George Washington in my class," she added.

"Mine too," Molly said.

"Why do they? He's not president anymore. President Roosevelt is."

"He was the father of our country," Molly said.

Rebecca smiled. "How could anybody be the father of a country?" she said.

"It only means he was the first president," Molly said, and turned back to her own work. She was having trouble getting started on her I Am an American Day composition. She wrote two or three sentences, then couldn't go on. After a while she gave up and went into the living room to read her library book. When Joey and Papa and Aunt Bessie came home, Molly repeated for them the episode in her sewing class. Soon, everyone sat down to a supper of meatballs and mashed potatoes.

"You sure gave us a scare last night, Rebecca," Joey said, smacking the bottom of the catsup bottle over his plate.

"Don't mention it," Mama said, picking up a bit of potato that Yaaki had dropped and putting it in his mouth.

Recalling the fright, Molly looked at her little sister. "She won't do that ever again. Will you?" she said.

Rebecca shook her head.

"By the way," Aunt Bessie said. "How was the play? You didn't tell us."

"I don't know," Rebecca said, looking up. "It was all in Jewish."

Everyone laughed.

"I didn't even notice it," Molly said.

"I understood one thing," Rebecca said. "The lady on the stage kept saying *prunes*, and every time she said it the audience started laughing."

Joey looked at Molly. "Sounds like a terrific play," he said, rolling his eyes.

"I have an idea," Papa said. "Rebecca's birthday is coming. Why should we wait? Why don't we give her a present now?"

Rebecca's eyes opened wide.

"Then she'll be disappointed when she doesn't get a present on her birthday," Molly said.

"No, I won't," Rebecca said.

"I'll tell you what," Aunt Bessie said. "I'll treat every-one to a meal at the Famous Restaurant on her birthday, the whole family."

"Wow!" Joey said.

Molly had been to a restaurant once, a Chinese res-taurant. She shuddered at the thought. It wasn't kosher. And she had gone with a girl from school, secretly, without the knowledge or permission of her parents. The food had made her sick to her stomach. Even now, the thought made her nauseous. But generally she liked the idea of eating in restaurants. And the thought of going to the Famous with her whole family excited her.

"So what would you like for a present?" Mama asked Rebecca.

Rebecca looked away and grew silent.

"Tell us," Papa said.

"Come on, Rebecca," Molly said, curious.

"Does it cost a million dollars?" Joey said.

Rebecca smiled but did not look up.

"Tell us, darling," Mama said.

"I don't know if he's Jewish," Rebecca said shyly.

"If who's Jewish?" Molly asked.

"Mickey Mouse," Rebecca said. "If he's Jewish, I'd like a Mickey Mouse watch."

"He looks Jewish to me," Aunt Bessie said.

Molly laughed with the rest.

Papa said he would bring Rebecca the Mickey Mouse watch when he came home from work tomorrow. Yaaki wanted a present too, so Joey made him a harmonica by putting toilet paper around a comb. Watching Yaaki hum noisily into the comb made Molly think of Eli, walking along and playing his harmonica. She held on to the thought, enjoying it.

Joey left after supper to meet his friends, and Molly and the rest of the family went into the living room to listen to Mayor La Guardia on the radio.

Molly sat on the arm of the sofa to hold the loose wire in back of the radio, and soon the mayor's high, squeaky voice was filling the room. New York had had blackout drills, to make the city dark in case the Germans came to attack. The mayor had hurt himself in a fall during a drill and said he was better now. He spoke about I Am an American Day, when the city and the schools put on programs about patriotism, and also said school children should be taught manners and cleanliness in addition to their other subjects.

The mayor's talk had given Molly an idea for her homework, and she went into the kitchen. She decided to write a poem instead of a composition. As she sat down at the table, the earlier worry arose. She saw in her mind's eye a picture of Beverly raised up in her seat. Then the picture changed and she saw Beverly in the sewing class, doubled over with laughter. Molly didn't think that if Beverly were going to tell on her she could have laughed so.

On a separate piece of paper, Molly worked out her rhymes. She decided to make the end of the poem funny. In case the poem wasn't any good, she could say it was only a joke. When she was through, she copied the finished poem onto a clean sheet:

I Am an American Day

President Roosevelt says, "God bless our fighting men."
Mrs. Roosevelt says, "We must all pitch in to do our part."
To be good Americans our parents give to the Red Cross
And buy U.S. War Bonds with a patriotic heart.

The children should also do something to help.
For the mayor's ideas let us give three cheers.
He says, "Be polite. Say thank you and please,
And also be sure to wash behind your ears."

54

6 New Shoes for Joey

It was pouring outside, but it was quiet and cozy in the living room. Molly sat on the couch reading her new library book, *Anne of Green Gables*. Joey, beside her, read the Sunday jokes, passing the pages he finished to Rebecca and Yaaki on the floor. Papa sat in the green chair, reading his paper.

Molly could hear Mama and Aunt Bessie talking in the kitchen. Now and then she glanced up, making a face against the rain. She read on to the end of the chapter, then, feeling restless, got up and went to the window to watch the rain. It fell in heavy splashes and left pools of water on the sidewalk.

"Some spring!" she said.

"It's not spring yet," Joey said. "Another few days."

Papa looked up from his paper. "When it rains this hard, it doesn't last long," he said.

Molly flopped back down on the couch again.

"Where's *Dick Tracy*?" Yaaki said.

"You read it already," Joey said.

"Oh," Yaaki said.

Molly thought about the book she was reading. Anne was an orphan. She lived with foster parents. Molly couldn't imagine growing up without her parents. It occurred to her that Tsippi was half an orphan. She had never asked Tsippi how that felt. Just then, to her amazement, the front door opened and Tsippi came in.

"I can't get over this," Molly said, straightening. "I was just thinking of you."

"Must be telepathy," Tsippi said.

Molly eyed her friend. "You came in this rain and you're not wet?" she said.

"My boots and umbrella are in the hall," Tsippi said.

"Did you see my watch, Tsippi?" Rebecca asked, holding up her wrist.

"Mickey Mouse," Tsippi said. "It's beautiful."

"He's Jewish," Rebecca said.

"He is?" Tsippi asked, looking at Molly.

"Aunt Bessie says so," Molly said and winked. She wanted to be alone with her friend. "Let's go in my room," she said, getting up.

"It's my room too," Rebecca said.

Molly gave her sister a look.

"And Aunt Bessie's," Rebecca added.

"Come on," Molly said, taking Tsippi by the hand.

They went into the next room and closed the door.

"Wait a minute," Tsippi said. "Why do we have to

sit here? My father's not going out today, on account of the rain. Let's go sit in the car. It's in front of the house."

The idea appealed to Molly. A car was a private place, and cozy, like a little house. "Let's go," she said.

They left the room, and as Molly took her coat from the hall closet, Tsippi went out into the hall to put on her boots.

"Where are you going?" Mama asked.

"Out," Molly said.

"In this rain?" Mama said.

"Tsippi was out in it and she didn't drown," Molly said. "Besides, she has an umbrella."

"Put on galoshes," Mama said.

"Ma, it's raining, not snowing," Molly said.

"The galoshes will keep your feet dry," Mama said.

"I'm only going up the block, not to the North Pole," Molly said.

"It takes only a second to get socked," Mama said.

"Not socked, *soaked*," Molly said, correcting her mother.

"What does it hurt you, Molly? Put them on," Aunt Bessie said.

Annoyed, and to end the conversation, Molly took the big galoshes from the closet and put them on, leaving the heavy clasps unfastened. Tsippi stood waiting for her in the hall.

"When the rain stops, come home," Mama said. "We're going to Thirteenth Avenue to buy shoes for Joey."

"I don't want the whole family coming," Joey called from the living room.

"Never mind—" Mama answered him from the kitchen.

Huddled together under the open umbrella, Molly and Tsippi hurried through the rain. Molly wished now that she had fastened the clasps on the galoshes. The sides flapped around, getting her legs wet.

They arrived at the car, opened the back door, and hurried inside. Tsippi closed the wet umbrella and put it on the floor.

"Whew," Molly said, unbuttoning her coat and glad to be inside. She listened to the rain falling on the rooftop. "I love that sound, don't you?" she said.

"Ummm," Tsippi said. "Especially when I'm inside."

Molly smiled at her friend and remembered the question she had about being an orphan. "Do you miss your real mother?" she asked, watching the rain splash on the windshield.

"I was little when she died," Tsippi said.

"Did you miss her when she died?"

"I cried all the time."

"Now you have a stepmother," Molly said.

Tsippi nodded.

"Do you like her?"

"My stepmother?"

"Um-hmm," Molly said.

"She's very good to me."

"Do you love her?"

Tsippi looked away. "Yes," she said, as if she were

thinking about it for the first time. "She's good to me," she repeated.

Molly wondered about Julie and her mother. Julie wasn't an orphan. But she had no father and lived only with her mother. "Do you think Julie loves her mother?" Molly asked.

"I do," Tsippi said.

"But her mother's so terrible."

"To us, but not to her," Tsippi said. "I never heard her say anything. I think she does love her mother," she added. As she faced Molly, she noticed something in back. "Look, cookies!" she said, reaching for a small cardboard box. She looked inside. "Fig cookies," she said, holding the open box up to Molly.

"Won't your father mind?" Molly asked, taking one.

"Naaah," Tsippi said. "We always have lots of cookies around."

The girls sat talking and eating fig cookies until the box was empty.

"Let's sing," Molly said.

"Okay, you start."

Molly picked a song she liked. "Mairzy dotes and doesy dotes," she began, and Tsippi joined in.

As they sat singing their favorite songs, the rain grew lighter and the day began to brighten.

"It stopped," Molly said.

"Your mother said to go home when it stopped."

"I know," Molly said. "You want to come with us? We're going to buy my brother shoes."

"I can't," Tsippi said. "But maybe I'll come over later to listen to the radio—if we don't have company, or anything."

Sorry to leave her cozy spot, Molly got out of the car. "See you later," she called, and headed down the street, her galoshes flapping from side to side.

As she crossed the avenue she saw Rebecca walking toward her.

"Where are you going?" Molly asked.

"I was coming to get you. We're going to Thirteenth Avenue," Rebecca said. "Was it nice in the car?" she added as they walked home.

"How did you know I was in the car?" Molly asked.

"I heard Tsippi say so."

"But you weren't in the room. Were you listening at the door? It's not nice to listen to other people's conversations," Molly said.

"I wasn't listening and I wasn't at the door," Rebecca said. "But my ears heard it anyhow."

Exasperated, Molly went inside and took off the galoshes. Everyone was dressed to go out and arguing with Joey.

"I don't see why the whole family has to come when I buy shoes," Joey said.

"Are you against families?" Papa said.

"No, but I'm not a baby. I'm in junior high. I'll be going to high school soon."

"Of course you're not a baby," Papa said. "You're

going to buy new shoes. We're going for a walk in that direction. Why shouldn't we all walk together?"

"What does it hurt, Joey?" Aunt Bessie asked.

Yaaki came up to Mama. "I'm all dressed," he said.

"I know. We all are," Mama said. "Come, let's go."

Molly and her family left the house and headed for Thirteenth Avenue. They spoke to each other as they went along. As if he were by himself, Joey walked alone in front of the group. Mama and Aunt Bessie, arm in arm, walked behind him with Rebecca. Papa pushed Yaaki's stroller and Molly walked with them.

"Doesn't it smell good after the rain?" Molly said, taking a deep breath of air.

"The sky is blue as anything," Mama said.

"These sneakers are falling apart," Joey said. "I really need a new pair."

"No more sneakers," Mama said. "You can't get them anymore, on account of the rubber."

"The rubber goes for the Army," Rebecca said, repeating a phrase she often heard.

"You'll get shoes with rubber soles," Mama said. "That way, you'll have sneakers for gym and new shoes for Passover."

"The gym teacher hates the rubber soles," Joey said. "They leave black marks on the floor."

"Too bad about him," Molly said from the rear.

At the store, Joey refused to go in if everyone went in with him.

"It's crazy," he said. "This is not a *bar mitzvah* or a party. I'm going to buy a pair of shoes. Why does every-one have to come in?"

"You want us to wait outside in the cold?" Mama said.

"It's not that cold," Joey said.

Molly felt sorry for her brother. He was older and she looked up to him, even if they sometimes fought.

"I'll wait outside," she said, to help. "Anyone going to keep me company?"

"I will," Rebecca said.

"I will too," Yaaki said.

"It's really not bad out," Aunt Bessie said, glancing at the weather. "I'll wait outside too."

"Let him go in alone," Papa said to Mama.

Mama opened her pocketbook and gave Joey money. "Here," she said. "Only don't buy the first pair they show you. Walk around in them first, and see if they fit."

Joey looked at Mama. "You can come in with me," he said.

"Fine, I'll wait outside," Papa said.

"You can come in too," Joey said.

Molly saw her brother glance at Aunt Bessie and knew he wouldn't be able to let her feel left out. "You shouldn't stay outside," he said.

They went to the door.

"If they're going, I want to go too," Rebecca said.

Joey made a face.

62

"I want to go with Papa," Yaaki said.

Molly was perfectly willing to help, but her plan hadn't worked, and she did not want to be left standing outside, alone.

"What am I, the wooden Indian in front of the cigar store?" she said.

"Okay, okay," Joey said. "Everybody come in," he added, opening the door.

Joey got new shoes that were brown with recycled rubber soles. Mama carried them home for him in a box so he could go meet his friends.

Sunday was delicatessen night, and everyone went to the delicatessen where Mama bought hot dogs and baked beans for supper.

Sunday was also the best radio night. George Burns and Gracie Allen, Eddie Cantor, Edgar Bergen and Charlie McCarthy, and others were on. After supper, everyone went into the living room to listen to the radio.

7 The Fig Cookies

The next morning, as Molly sat at the breakfast table, Tsippi burst in.

"You'll never guess what," she said, staring at Molly.

"What?" Molly said, waiting to hear more.

"I hate to tell you," Tsippi said.

"Tell me what?"

"Those fig cookies we ate yesterday?"

"Your father was mad?"

"And how! But I hate to tell you why."

Molly could not imagine what Tsippi was talking about. She stared at her friend.

"The fig cookies had worms inside!" Tsippi said.

"What!" Molly cried.

"My father went down to the car this morning to get the box," Tsippi said. "He was going to sue the company." She leaned over the table wide-eyed. "We ate the evidence," she said. "We ate the worms!"

Molly felt her stomach lurch.

Mama looked perplexed. "The fig cookies you ate had worms?" she asked.

Tsippi nodded, a look of disgust on her face.

"I don't believe it," Molly said, holding her belly.

"You better believe it," Tsippi said, grabbing her own belly.

Yaaki laughed.

"Are worms kosher?" Rebecca asked.

"Ugh! Cut it out!" Molly said, shoving the food away from herself and getting up from the table. She and Tsippi stared at each other, speechless.

"Are we going to die?" Molly asked.

"*Shah! Ptu!*" Mama said, spitting the notion away. "Don't say such things."

"No," Tsippi said. "My father says some people eat worms all the time. But he sure was mad at us for eating the evidence," she added.

Molly stood clutching herself.

"I'll never eat"—she couldn't get the words 'fig cookies' past her lips—"those things again as long as I live," she said.

Rebecca took her book and pencil box and went to the door.

"We better go," Tsippi said.

"I can't believe it," Molly said, getting her books. "So long," she called in a weak voice, fighting off a wave of nausea.

"So long," Yaaki answered.

"See you for lunch," Mama said.

"Ma!" Molly cried, spinning around. "How can you talk about food at a time like this?"

"Who said anything about food?" Mama said. "I said, 'See you for lunch.' "

"Ma! Honestly!" Molly said. "If I didn't know you were my mother, I'd think you were trying to make me sick."

"Go, already," Mama said. "And take the worms with you."

Molly gave her mother a look of disgust and turned to Tsippi. "Let's go," she said weakly, showing her friend the pain and nausea on her face.

8 An Empty Lap

Molly glanced at the clock on the refrigerator, wondering what was keeping Tsippi. The day was pleasant and warm, and Molly was glad spring had come. The kitchen window was open, and as she ate her breakfast she listened to the welcome sound of neighbors talking to each other from their courtyard windows.

"I love the warm weather," she said. "The first thing I heard when I opened my eyes this morning was a bird singing."

"I didn't hear anything," Rebecca said.

"Maybe you can't hear it from your side of the bed."

Rebecca gave Molly a long look. "Why don't we go to school? Where's Tsippi?"

"Let's wait another couple of minutes," Molly said, sipping slowly from her cocoa. She watched Mama open the cupboard and begin sweeping the shelves with a little brush.

"I thought you cleaned there," Molly said.

"I did. Now I'm really cleaning."

Molly shrugged. Mama had been saying such things all week. Passover started tonight, and Mama had been cleaning for days. On Passover, Jews did not eat bread, only matzo, a flat, large biscuit. No bread, not even a crumb, was supposed to remain in the house. And Mama was sweeping away every crumb.

"I don't want you coming home for lunch and making crumbs," Mama said. "I made sandwiches for you to eat in school."

"I'm glad," Rebecca said. "I like to eat lunch in school."

"What's in the sandwich, Ma?" Molly asked.

"Cream cheese and jelly," Mama said.

Molly hid the face she was making from Mama and glanced at the clock again.

"Looks like Tsippi got lost," she said.

"Maybe she's sick," Rebecca said.

"That wouldn't stop her," Molly said. "Let's go."

Mama took the lunches from the refrigerator and gave each girl a bag. She glanced into the courtyard.

"It is a beautiful day," she said. "Soon the trees will be green and we'll have dandelins."

"Dandelions, Ma," Molly said, correcting her mother.

"Why is lion in the name if it's a flower?" Rebecca asked.

Molly didn't know. "I'll ask Miss Smith," she said. "She knows all about flowers."

" 'Bye, Yaaki," Rebecca called.

Yaaki came in from the living room and stood with a

raised hand, waving. He looked so cute to Molly, she had to kiss him.

"Uuu—I'm going to give you a big kiss," she said, heading for him.

"You gave me one already," he said.

"That was a winter kiss. It's spring now. Hear the birds? This will be for spring." Molly kept talking to keep him from leaving, and managed to plant a kiss on his cheek before he ducked out of the way.

"Happy spring," she called, going out the door with Rebecca.

"I can't imagine what happened to Tsippi today," Molly said, half to herself, as they walked up the street.

"There she is," Rebecca said.

"Where?" Molly asked, looking about.

"On the corner, across the way," Rebecca said, pointing.

Molly looked and saw Tsippi talking to a boy. Surprised, she slowed down, wondering if Tsippi would notice her. As she walked she strained to keep Tsippi in the corner of her eye.

"Molly!" Tsippi called, and came running.

"His father is a friend of my father," Tsippi said, falling in with Molly and Rebecca and pushing her glasses up on her nose.

"Who?" Molly asked, as if she didn't know.

"That boy," Tsippi said, nodding.

"What boy?" Molly asked, looking about.

"The one she was talking to," Rebecca said.

Molly pretended not to hear.

"Alan is his name," Tsippi said, as the girls turned into the schoolyard. "His father brought him over to our house the other night."

"Oh," Molly said, realizing she was jealous and hating to admit it to herself.

In class Miss Smith collected the homework. She reminded the class of the final test coming up next week before beginning the arithmetic lesson. Molly shuddered. She glanced at Beverly, who was stretching her fingers, almost in Molly's face. Molly wondered if it meant anything. It was hard to tell with Beverly. The old question arose for Molly. Had she been right in thinking that Beverly had seen nothing? Or was she just fooling herself? Molly felt uneasy again. And ashamed.

When the lunch bell rang, Molly went down to the cafeteria with her sandwich. She almost never ate in school. Some girls ate there all the time. She sat at a table with some girls she knew and was glad to get back to class when lunch was over.

Miss Smith had graded the compositions the class had written yesterday afternoon. She went around the room, giving them out. Molly waited for hers. She watched the teacher walk from desk to desk, and pass her by each time.

"I've held out one composition," Miss Smith said, returning to her desk.

The announcement gave Molly a start. It had to be hers. She was the only one who hadn't received a paper back. She had written about orphans. Had she said something dumb, or done something wrong?

"I kept it," Miss Smith said, "because I wanted everyone to hear it. It's called 'An Empty Lap,' and it's about an orphan."

Molly's heart was beating like a hammer. It *was* hers!

Molly listened with embarrassment, then with pleasure, as Miss Smith read her composition aloud. It was about a lonely orphan and a lonely, childless couple. The couple adopted the girl, and they loved each other and were happy. Now the orphan had two laps to sit in. And the previously empty laps of her parents were filled. Molly could feel her ears burning and knew they were red. She knew Tsippi, who sat behind her, could see them. She hoped Eli sat too far back for that.

Miss Smith flashed Molly a smile as she dropped the paper on her desk.

Molly heard a soft hiss come from her seatmate. She glanced at Beverly and saw a look of hatred. Beverly quickly changed the expression on her face and stretched her lips into a smile.

Miss Smith went to the front of the room and spoke.

"I couldn't find any fault with Molly's composition," she said. "Even so, I have not given her one hundred but ninety-eight, because nothing is perfect. Not even that most perfect flower—the rose."

Much as Molly enjoyed the compliment, she thought the teacher had said enough. She wanted to change the subject. She remembered Rebecca's question of the morning and raised her hand. Miss Smith liked to answer questions about flowers.

"My little sister asked me this morning why the word lion was in dandelion," Molly said.

"Dandelion is a French word—or series of French words," the teacher said. She picked up a piece of chalk and wrote: *dent de lion*. "*Dent* means tooth," she said. "*Leeyon* is lion in French. The flower was given its name because its leaves resemble lion's teeth."

"Thank you, Miss Smith," Molly said, feeling a flood of love and admiration for the teacher and copying the words into her notebook. She was glad she had decided to take French.

Miss Smith began to speak about the Jewish holiday of Passover, telling the class it started tonight. She asked for volunteers to explain the meaning. Eli went to the front and told how the Jewish slaves had suffered in Egypt and how Moses had freed them.

As he spoke Molly began to look forward to the *seder*, the banquet ceremony, that would take place at her house tonight. The relatives were coming. She hadn't seen her cousins Mordi and Selma for a long time.

As the class let out, Tsippi came over to Molly. "You should have seen your ears," Tsippi said.

"I know," Molly smiled. "I could feel them."

"Congratulations on the composition, Molly," Eli said as he ran by.

"That was a good speech you gave," Molly called after him, hoping Tsippi didn't notice that she was blushing.

Rebecca was waiting for Molly downstairs. Tsippi left the girls at the gate, and Molly and Rebecca walked on home. Molly remembered the arithmetic test coming up on Monday but brushed the thought away. She didn't want to think about it now. She had too many nice things to think about—Miss Smith's compliment, Eli's, the *seder* tonight. She felt dreamy as she walked along.

9 *The* Seder

Molly gasped as she opened the kitchen door. The room had been transformed. The table had been made twice as long with a bridge table added at either end. It was covered with a white cloth and looked beautiful, set with matching dishes, shiny silverware, and wine glasses.

Papa walked around the table, placing a *Haggadah*, a little book that told the Passover story and was read during the *seder*, beside each plate.

"It looks like a palace, Ma," Molly said.

"I helped," Papa said.

"Me too," Aunt Bessie said from the sideboard, where she was chopping onions and crying.

Joey came in from the outside.

"I suppose you did too," Molly said.

"Did what?" he asked.

"Never mind, as Mama says," Molly answered, and went to put her books away.

When she came back into the kitchen, Papa and Rebecca were checking to see that all the symbolic foods were present on the table.

"The wine, which stands for joy," Papa said. "And the matzo, the bread the Israelite slaves ate when they left Egypt, which stands for freedom."

"What does the tablecloth stand for?" Molly asked, feeling lighthearted.

"Smart aleck!" Joey said.

"It stands for pretty," Mama said.

Molly thought it *was* pretty. She stood counting the chairs and, in her mind, matched one up to each person who was coming. A seder was so much fun. Her friend Julie never went anywhere and hardly ever had fun. She wished Julie could come to the seder.

"There's only ten chairs," she said.

"*Oy!*" Mama said, slapping her face. "Did we forget somebody?"

"There's five of us, plus Yaaki in his highchair," Molly said, counting aloud. "Aunt Bessie is six. And four in Aunt Esther's family."

"That's ten, what's wrong?" Papa said.

"But we're supposed to invite a stranger for Passover," Molly said. Julie wasn't a real stranger. But she wasn't a member of the family either. Julie loved holiday celebrations.

"We invite a stranger if we know one," Mama said. "But nowhere is it written that we have to go in the street looking for one."

"Julie is a stranger," Molly said.

"Shirley is a stranger too," Rebecca said.

"You can't invite Shirley and not her mother," Mama said. "All right, invite your strangers. I'll borrow chairs," she added.

"Let's hope Joey doesn't know any strangers," Molly heard Mama say as she ran out to tell Julie.

All those invited had agreed to come. Molly washed up and put on a pretty plaid dress, a hand-me-down from the rich cousins. She reminded herself that she was supposed to start taking better care of her appearance and made herself stand in front of the mirror and comb her hair.

"Everyone looks so nice," she said, going into the kitchen and seeing her family all dressed up and Yaaki in a new little suit.

The company arrived within minutes of each other— Shirley and her mother, then Julie, looking nice, with her hair combed and held in place by a barrette, and a moment later, Aunt Esther, her husband, Julius, and Molly's cousins, Selma and Mordi. Selma was the center of attraction. She was in the Women's Army Auxiliary Corps, the WAAC, and was wearing her uniform.

"I bet the whole neighborhood was staring at you," Molly said.

"From their windows and from their stoops, as Winston Churchill might say," Selma said with a smile.

Molly sidled up to Mordi and touched shoulders with him. "You were a little shrimp the last time I saw you," she said. "You're as tall as me!"

Mordi beamed.

Rebecca showed everyone her Micky Mouse watch, and Molly introduced her cousins to her friends.

"Hi," Mordi said. "You m-m-might as w-well f-f-find out r-right away. I st-stutter."

"A boy in my class stutters too," Julie said.

Shirley kept staring at Selma. "How is it to be in the army?" she asked.

"There's a war on. A person has to do something," Selma said.

Molly saw that Selma had changed. Her cousin used to be a Communist. She used to sound as if she were making a speech.

"Come, everyone," Papa called. "Mama is going to light the candles."

Everyone stood watching as Mama kindled the candles and said the holiday blessing.

"Amen," Molly answered with the others, noticing that Julie didn't say anything.

"Take seats," Papa said, going around the table and pouring wine for the adults and grape juice for the children.

Molly, sitting between Julie and her cousin Selma, was thrilled to see Papa pour wine in her glass and also in Julie's. Molly told Julie this was the first year she was receiving wine, not grape juice, and the girls exchanged smiles of pleasure.

"Will I get wine next year?" Rebecca asked from the

other side of the table, seated next to Shirley and her mother.

"We'll see," Papa said, returning to his place at the head of the table. Mama, Yaaki, and Joey were at that end too. Aunt Esther and her family sat at the other end.

"When I nudge you, say amen," Molly whispered to Julie.

Papa lifted his wine glass and recited the wine blessing: *"Baruk ata Adonai, Elohenu melek ha'olam, boreh pri hagafen."* (Praises are due you, Lord, our God, ruler of the universe, who created the fruit of the vine.)

"Amen," Molly sang out with the others, nudging Julie.

The kitchen window was open, and a din was suddenly heard in the courtyard. The words "Jews!"— "War!"—"Nazis!" hung on the air. Molly and the others around the table grew silent as Papa went to the window. "What is it?" Papa called.

"Turn on the radio," a voice answered.

As everyone got up from the table, Joey ran into the living room to turn on the set.

"It's so exciting," Julie said to Molly, blowing the hair out of her eyes. "Nothing ever happens in my house."

"Well, it's not exactly happening *in* my house—" Molly said.

"I mean the *seder* and all—"

"Shhh," Mama said as the announcer's voice came up.

. . . Jews of the Warsaw Ghetto revolted when German tanks and artillery surrounded the area. With homemade hand grenades, handguns, and broken glass, the starving and sick Jews—men, women, and children—struck back against the German slave masters.

Everyone looked at Selma because she was in uniform.

"What does it mean?" Uncle Julius asked.

"Just what he said," Selma answered. "The Germans surrounded the ghetto, to kill the Jews. The Jews are fighting back."

"They have no chance," Papa said.

"No—" Selma said.

"God save and bless our people," Aunt Esther said.

"Amen and amen," Mama said. "Come, everyone," she added a moment later, returning to the kitchen. "We have a *seder*."

"Let's sit down, Julie," Molly said, taking her friend by the hand.

"Page two," Papa said, opening his *Haggadah*.

Molly opened her book and Julie's, and showed Julie where everyone would read from. She glanced around the table, enjoying the sight of so many people and everyone looking so nice for the holiday.

Papa said, "We praise your name, God, in behalf of our people who are fighting in Warsaw tonight, and add our pleas for salvation to theirs."

Molly felt a chill. "Amen," she answered with the others, nudging Julie.

"We read together," Papa said. And everyone read: "Praises are due you, Lord our God, ruler of the universe, who has given us life, kept us safe, and brought us to this holy season."

"We sip wine now," Papa said, drinking from his glass. "Or grape juice," he added, nodding at Rebecca and Mordi.

"I'm afraid to get drunk," Aunt Esther said, smiling at her glass.

"Get out," Aunt Bessie said, laughing.

"Go ahead, drink it, it'll put hair on your chest," Uncle Julius said.

Molly saw Selma make a face behind her glass. Julius, Aunt Esther's new husband, was a nice man but his jokes were terrible. Molly noticed Julie staring at her glass.

"Did you drink?" Molly asked.

Julie shook her head. "I'm afraid. I don't want to get drunk either."

"Go ahead," Molly said. "Besides, you have to. That's the law. You're supposed to have a good time."

Julie hesitantly brought the glass to her lips and took a small sip. She looked proud as she put the glass down and licked her lips.

"Before us," Papa said, "on the holiday tray, are the symbolic foods of this holiday. The egg stands for life.

Who knows what the other foods stand for?"

Molly knew what the mashed apples and nuts stood for. "The *haroset* stands for the bricks the ancient Jews made when they were slaves in Egypt," she said.

"Joey, what about the *maror*, the bitter herb?" Papa said.

"That stands for the bitter lives of the slaves," Joey said.

"I used to know what the lamb bone stands for, but I forgot," Aunt Bessie said, covering her face with her hand to show she was embarrassed.

"For the lamb that used to be sacrificed in ancient times," Papa said.

"The celery stands for spring, doesn't it?" Selma asked.

"It stands for indigestion," Uncle Julius said.

"Doesn't it stand for the food that God puts in the earth, for us to eat?" Shirley said.

Papa nodded.

"I don't know what anything stands for," Julie said. "This is my first *seder*."

"I d-d-don't know either," Mordi said.

"Don't you know what the salt water stands for?" Rebecca asked.

"The ocean?" Mordi said.

Everyone laughed.

"The tears of the Jewish slaves," Rebecca said.

"A pretty smart bunch, huh, Yaaki?" Papa said to bring the baby into the conversation.

"When is the food?" Yaaki said. And everyone laughed.

Molly was glad to see the other "strangers," Shirley and her mother, smiling and enjoying themselves.

"The youngest person now asks the four questions," Papa said. "Yaaki is the youngest, but he can't read yet. So Rebecca and Mordi will ask two questions each."

"I'll go first," Rebecca said. Reading where Shirley showed her, she said, "Why is this night different from other nights?"

Molly and the others read the answer, "Because on other nights we eat both matzo *and* bread, and on this night only matzo."

"Why do we eat many herbs on other nights and on this night only bitter herbs?" Rebecca read.

"To recall the bitter lives of our ancestors, who were slaves in Egypt," Molly answered with the others.

Mordi read the last two questions: "Why on other n-n-nights d-do we d-dip n-not even once, and on th-this n-n-night we d-dip twice?"

"We dip celery in the salt water to celebrate the spring crops," Molly answered with the others, "and dip parsley in the sweet *haroset* to show hope."

Mordi leaned back in his chair. "Why on other n-nights d-do we s-sit up to eat, b-b-but re-re-recline on th-this night?"

"Because in ancient times free people reclined when they ate, and on this night our slave ancestors became free," Molly answered with the others.

Julie smiled at Molly to show her pleasure. The sounds of other *seders* could be heard in the courtyard. Molly's heart was full of gladness. With all the bad news in Europe, she was happy to see that Jews could have a good time too.

10   *Clean Hands*

As the holiday excitement receded, Molly found herself worrying about Beverly again. She had convinced herself that she was safe. But she wasn't a hundred percent sure. The more she thought about it, the less sure she became. It seemed to her, as she thought back, that Miss Smith had hardly looked at her since the last test. Maybe Beverly *had* seen Molly's hand. And maybe Beverly, being Beverly, *had* told.

On Sunday, Molly went walking with the girls. When she and Tsippi were alone she spoke of her fears. Tsippi kept trying to reassure Molly. Molly's mood kept changing. One moment she was reassured, then she was worried again.

"Look," Tsippi said as they walked along. "You know Miss Smith. If Beverly saw, she would have told the teacher. And Miss Smith would have talked to you about it. Or she would have made some kind of speech in front of the whole class about cheating—or something."

Molly thought that was true.

"It's hard work to cheat," Molly said as they arrived in front of her house. "You have to watch every step."

"I know," Tsippi said.

"It takes away a person's honor," Molly said.

Tsippi nodded.

"I—I'm not going to cheat tomorrow—it's too aggravating," Molly said, hoping she meant it.

Inside, Molly took out her arithmetic book and sat down at the kitchen table to study. Mama was on the other side of the table, studying her citizenship book.

Molly turned to the fractions and looked over the printed material. She studied the example that was given: "A girl had five yards of material. Her dress pattern called for $2\frac{3}{4}$ yards. How many yards would be left after she made the dress?" The answer was $2\frac{1}{4}$. It was worked out. The book showed how to check, to see that the answer was right.

As Molly thought about it, she didn't see how she could pass without cheating. She was bad in arithmetic, but she was horrible in fractions. If she just put that one example on her hand, it would help a lot. She would put just that, nothing else.

She closed the book and went to the closet to look for a substitute good-luck dress that she could wear for the test. Nothing she took out felt lucky to her. She decided to wear the ruined pink dress but couldn't find it. She went into the kitchen, wondering if Mama knew where it was.

"My hand feels like it's on fire. My legs won't move. I feel like I'm in prison."

"What are you going to do?"

Molly burned with shame as she thought of Miss Smith, and of all the tiny Miss Smiths with pitchforks parading around her thoughts last night.

"You go in," she said.

"Good luck on the test," Tsippi called, and went in.

Molly found herself unstuck as she turned and crossed the hall. She went into the girls' bathroom, opened the sink faucet, and put her hand under the running water. As the blue ink was washed away, a sense of freedom came over her. She smiled down at her clean, pink hand. "If I fail, I fail," she thought and went back to class.

She waved her hand at Tsippi, wiggling her fingers proudly as she took her seat. Beverly was holding her pen in her hand like a fork, as if she were waiting for food. As Molly sat down she felt Beverly wriggle closer and closer to her, and she knew the girl was trying to get a glimpse of her hand.

Molly thought she would tease Beverly. She would act as if she were cheating. She opened her left hand loosely on her desk. Then, as if there were something written on her palm, she sent her glance there and quickly flicked her hand flat down on the desk.

She could not believe her eyes. Beverly went to speak to the teacher. Molly knew Beverly's tricks. Beverly acted as if she were asking for permission to go to the bathroom. But she didn't have to ask for permission to leave the room. The starting bell hadn't rung yet. Beverly left, and soon returned. She slid back into her seat, and picked up her pen again, the picture of innocence.

A moment or two later, the bell rang and Miss Smith closed the door. She stepped to the front of the room and folded her hands in front of herself.

"We will not have the arithmetic test this morning," she said.

Molly's heart skipped a beat. She could hear a gasp of surprise escape from Beverly.

Miss Smith smiled as cries of "Yay!" and "Hooray!" rose up from the back. "I did not say we weren't having the test at all," she said. "We will have it this after-noon."

"Why can't we have it now? We might forget," a voice called.

"Yeah, let's get it over with," another voice said.

"We will have history this morning," Miss Smith said, bringing the subject to an end.

Molly was shaking. Beverly *had* told. Molly felt the teacher had done it for her sake. She could feel it in her bones. The teacher probably didn't know whether to believe Beverly or not. But in case it were true, she was sending Molly a warning.

Molly wanted Miss Smith to know that she didn't have to postpone the test. To show the teacher that she had no intention of cheating, that her hands were clean, Molly rested both hands on her desk, palms up. It was a funny position, but she didn't care. She wanted Miss Smith to see her clean hands as she went by. Miss Smith did. Beverly did too. Beverly had been made out to be a liar. She turned purple and began bouncing around in her seat and chewing on a pencil. Molly enjoyed Beverly's distress. Hands open on her desk, she listened as Miss Smith told about the unfairness of taxation without representation.

Later, when the lunch bell rang, Molly and Tsippi left the room together.

"I wonder why she postponed the test," Tsippi said as they went down the stairs.

Molly looked at her friend. "Did you see Beverly go up to the teacher before the class?" she asked.

Tsippi nodded.

"I saw her trying to look at my hand. To spite her, I pretended I was cheating. She saw me looking at my hand and went to tell the teacher!"

"No!" Tsippi said.

"I know it sounds conceited," Molly said, embarrassed. "But I think she postponed the test on account of me, as a warning."

Tsippi shook her head. "Can you beat that?" she said with a smile.

Molly felt as if she were walking on air as she and Rebecca went home for lunch. Yaaki was in his highchair, "playing" his comb. Molly gave him a kiss as she sat down at the table. She ate, too exhilarated to know or care what she was putting into her mouth.

"Ma," Rebecca said, "you don't have to give me a penny for milk tomorrow. We're not having any."

"Why, is there a milk shortage?" Mama asked.

"Not the milk, the containers," Rebecca said.

"Why so quiet?" Mama asked Molly.

Molly wanted to be left alone. "We're having the arithmetic test this afternoon," she said by way of explanation.

"You'll pass, don't worry," Rebecca said.

Molly gave her little sister a smile. Mama removed Yaaki from the chair and set him on the floor. "Go play in the living room," she said. "Never mind," she added, turning to Molly.

"Never mind what?" Molly asked.

"A person doesn't have to be good in everything. No one is a jerk of all trades."

Molly laughed. She wondered if Mama had read that expression in her citizenship book. "Not jerk, Ma, jack."

Molly had a talk with herself as she walked back to school. She would fail the test, that was for sure. "So I fail," she said. "It's not the end of the world. It's better to fail than to be caught cheating and branded a cheat for the rest of my life. This way, I still have my honor. And"—the words *teacher's pet* came to mind, but she didn't want to act conceited—"Miss Smith still likes me," she said.

Eli was playing ball in the school yard. Molly stopped to watch him for a moment, then went inside. She nodded to Tsippi and took her seat. She could feel Beverly staring at her. Molly pretended to be thinking about something. Then she flung her hands open in front of Beverly's face and said, "Boo!" Molly laughed as Beverly gave her a look of disgust and turned away.

The sight of the stack of tests Miss Smith had placed on her desk changed Molly's mood and made her nervous. She reached up and touched the pink flower on her collar for good luck.

Eli ran by on his way to his seat. "Hi," he said, disappearing up the aisle. Molly looked after him, pleased that he had spoken to her.

The starting bell rang, and Miss Smith went to close the door. She took the tests from her desk and gave a batch to the first person in each row to pass back. Molly made sure, as she took the batch for her row, to display her clean hands. Beside her, Beverly was already working away.

Molly looked over the first problem. "Change the following fractions to decimals: $\frac{1}{4}$, $\frac{2}{5}$, $\frac{3}{25}$, $\frac{1}{20}$."

The room was silent. She thought she remembered how to do that. She heard the scratch of pens. She dipped her own pen in the ink, wrote her name at the top of the sheet, and began.

A hand suddenly came down on her shoulder. Startled, Molly looked up. Miss Smith smiled at her and walked away. Fighting back tears of gratitude and love, Molly worked on, tackling some problems, puzzling over others, skipping those that were too hard to do.

"Time!" Miss Smith called.

Molly and the others brought their tests to the front.

Miss Smith stood at the side of her desk and said, "When you were small, your mothers gave you chocolate to take with your castor oil. I don't have chocolate, but I have a reward for you too." She smiled. "Instead of the next study period, you can go out and play or go home."

Hoorays filled the room.

"Of course, if anyone wants to stay for study—I'll be here," Miss Smith said.

Loud but fake groans filled the room.

At the sound of the bell, everyone ran to the door. Molly wanted to say something to the teacher, but she didn't know what. She waited until she saw the teacher finish speaking to a girl, then went up to her and said, "I hope you have a nice afternoon, Miss Smith," and hurried out.

"How do you think you did?" Tsippi asked Molly in the hall.

"I'm sure I failed," Molly said. "All those fractions. So I won't be a jerk of all trades, as my mother says," she added.

Tsippi laughed.

Molly was making jokes but, deep down, she was hurting. She felt good and noble because she hadn't cheated this last time. She was sad because she would not be going into the RA with Tsippi and the other girls. Hurt as she was, she decided to keep her pain to herself.

It made her feel brave. And a quiet, warm feeling of self-respect came over her.

"Let's sit in the school yard," Tsippi said. "We don't have to go home yet."

The girls went to the ledge along the gate and sat down.

Molly sighed. "At last it's over," she said, resting the back of her head against the gate and feeling like a heroine in the movies.

"Molly," Tsippi said. "Remember that boy I was talking to that day?"

Molly remembered and nodded.

Tsippi bit her lip. "You're my best friend, and you'll be my best friend for the rest of my life," she said.

Molly knew that but wondered why Tsippi was suddenly saying so. "Best friends forever," she said, changing the words of the club motto to suit the occasion.

"He goes to another school," Tsippi said. "He's graduating in June too."

Wondering what Tsippi was getting at, Molly waited for her to say more.

"That boy—Alan is his name—" Tsippi said. "His friend is taking a girl to the Fox, to see *For Whom the Bell Tolls* with Ingrid Bergman. For graduation," she added, nodding her head. She bit her lip and smiled shyly. "Alan asked me. I'm going too," she said.

Molly's feelings clashed. She was glad for Tsippi, but

also jealous. "The Fox is far—you have to take a bus, don't you?" she said to say something.

Tsippi nodded.

"That's nice," Molly said, hoping she looked sincere.

11 *A Star Is Born*

Molly sat at the edge of her seat. Miss Smith had said she would give out the marked tests at the end of the day, and according to the clock on the wall, the end of the day was near. Molly's heart sank when Miss Smith went to the desk, where the tests lay in a batch.

"As a class, you didn't do too badly," she said, walking around, putting a test on each desk, facedown. "Three failed," the teacher added, "a good number were on the border, and the rest passed."

Molly saw Beverly grin as Beverly looked at her test mark. Molly felt small as Miss Smith stopped at her desk and dropped a sheet. Molly knew what was written there without looking. Even so, she turned the sheet up and glanced at it. Although she was prepared for the F, she still felt crushed when she looked at it. There was some other writing on the page. "Congratulations," she read. "Your school average over the years admits you to the RA." She didn't know whether to laugh or cry. "Tsippi!" she called, turning toward the aisle, away from Beverly. "I made it," she said, forming the words with her lips.

"Me too," Tsippi said with her lips, and made a V-for-victory sign with her fingers.

Molly could hardly sit still as Miss Smith went to the front of the room to remind the class about the graduation rehearsal coming up, and the picture-taking that would follow.

"A picture lasts forever," the teacher said. "So look your best."

When the bell rang, Molly motioned Tsippi to hurry and ran to the door.

"You passed," Tsippi said, looking pleased.

"No, I failed," Molly said. "I meant the RA," she added, almost jumping with excitement.

"Great! Me too," Tsippi said. The girls put their arms around one another as they walked down the hall.

"Let's see what happened with the other girls," Molly said as they went down the stairs.

They had arranged to meet the girls in the school yard after class, and they hurried to the ledge. As they sat waiting, their excitement about making the RA dwindled, and they began to discuss the bad features.

"It's not easy, doing a year's work in half a year," Molly said.

"Don't I know it?" Tsippi said.

"I bet we won't have time to do anything."

"We'll be lucky if we can take a walk."

"If we think we had a lot of homework in elementary school, just wait," Molly said. The school yard was filling up, and she saw the girls as she looked up.

"Here they are," she said. "They look happy. They must have good news too."

"We made the RA!" Little Naomi said, grinning.

"All of us," Big Naomi said, taking in Lily and Lila with a nod.

"We did too," Molly said, glancing at Tsippi.

"We could tell from your faces," Lily said. She made a cushion of her books and sat down on the ground. The other girls did the same.

"Boy," Lily said, "I never thought I'd make it."

"What about me?" Lila said. "Lousy in spelling, lousy in composition." She rolled her eyes. "It's a miracle."

Molly felt a wave of happiness wash over her. She felt love for everyone, even Alan, the boy with whom Tsippi had a date.

"And what about me, lousy in arithmetic?" she said. "They go by averages," she added, thinking she might have made the RA even if she hadn't cheated on the first two tests, and sorry and ashamed that she had.

"Montauk!" Tsippi said, speaking the name of the junior high school with a sigh.

Molly's happiness knew no bounds. "We are not elementary-school girls anymore," she said, feeling grown up.

"Wouldn't it be great if we all end up in the same class in Montauk?" Lily said.

"We won't," Molly said. "They don't do that. Kids from different elementary schools come there, and they try to mix them up. My brother Joey knew two people in his class when he started," she added. "That's all."

"That's the part that scares me," Lily said. "Not knowing anybody."

"Yeah," Little Naomi said, looking about the crowded schoolyard. "Here, we know the whole school."

"So what?" Molly said. "We're not in the same class here, and we're still best friends." She took the hands of the two girls closest to her. The other girls also joined hands.

"Friends forever!" Molly said.

"Friends forever!" the girls repeated.

"Here comes Julie," Molly said, and the girls dropped hands. "Don't say anything about the RA, in case she didn't make it," Molly added.

"She didn't," Big Naomi said. "I don't even know if she got promoted."

"From her face, she did," Molly said.

Julie ran up, blowing the hair out of her eyes. "I passed, thank God," she said.

"Great!" Molly said.

"I was really worried," Julie said. "I missed a lot of classes, on account of my mother being sick."

"Sit down," Molly said, moving over on the ledge, making room for Julie.

Molly and the girls sat awhile longer, talking about the next term, exaggerating the worries they expected

100

to face in the RA for Julie's sake; then everyone parted to go home. Molly ran all the way.

"Guess what!" she said, stepping into the kitchen. Mama, Rebecca, and Yaaki were having an afternoon snack at the table. She did not wait for an answer. "I made the RA!" she said, bursting with happiness.

"Wonderful!" Mama said, taking Molly's hand and kissing it.

Rebecca beamed. "Hooray for Molly," she said.

"What is it?" Yaaki asked.

"She got promoted, you're too young to understand," Rebecca said.

Yaaki put his comb to his lips and started playing.

"We should do something to celebrate," Mama said.

"Naah," Molly said, pleased at the suggestion.

"You want milk and cookies?" Mama asked.

The milk and cookies on the table seemed babyish to Molly suddenly.

"Is there any coffee left from the morning?" she said, as Papa or Aunt Bessie might ask.

Mama looked surprised. "Since when do you drink coffee?"

"Since today," Molly said. "I'm going into junior high."

"There is," Mama said, getting up. "I'll heat it."

Molly was still overflowing with feelings of love. "Give me a kiss," she said, sitting down next to Yaaki.

He did not look at her and did not answer, but continued playing his comb.

"Just a little one," she said, squeezing his chubby leg.

He leaned forward a little, kissed the air, and continued playing.

Molly lifted the cup of coffee Mama put before her and took a sip. It tasted bitter and she wasn't sure that she liked it, but she drank it anyhow and became aware that Mama was watching her.

"What's the matter?" Molly asked.

"I never saw you drink coffee before," Mama said.

"Am I doing it wrong?" Molly asked.

"No," Mama said.

All the excitement had made Molly hungry, and now she wanted something to eat. She brought the butter and a slice of bread to the table. She remembered tasting salty butter at Little Naomi's house for the first time, and liking it.

"Why don't we ever have salty butter?" she said, buttering the bread.

"Sweet is better," Mama said.

"But why can't we have it? My friends all have it," Molly said.

"If your friends had pneumonia, would you want pneumonia too?" Mama said.

"Ma! Why do you have to be like that?" Molly said.

"Like what?" Mama said, taking a sip of tea.

Molly finished her snack and went outside to sit on the stoop so she could be alone with her thoughts. She stretched her legs out in front of herself, rested her head against the wall of the house, and let her thoughts wander over the events of the day. Her heart stood still as she caught sight of Eli, on the other side of the street. He was delivering something for the tailor, walking along with a suit on a hanger slung over his shoulder and playing his harmonica.

Molly took her legs down and sat in a more ladylike position, in case he looked her way. He didn't though. He walked on, playing. She watched him until he was out of sight, then went inside.

Mama was listening to Jeanette MacDonald and Nelson Eddy on the radio. Feeling dreamy, Molly sat down beside her. Yaaki was on the floor, playing his comb.

"Yaaki," Mama said. "Go play in the kitchen—I'm trying to listen."

Yaaki got up and went into the kitchen.

Molly put her head on Mama's shoulder and listened to the words of "Indian Love Call," thinking of Eli. Rebecca came in and also sat down in the living room to listen.

"And now," the announcer said, "Jan Peerce, singing that heartbreaking aria 'Ridi, Pagliaccio.' Laugh, clown."

Molly loved that aria. Mama and Rebecca did too. It was in Italian and they did not understand a word, but the singer's voice was choked with sadness, and they were all moved to tears and sat crying.

"Who died?" Joey asked, as he came home from school.

"*Uuu,* you have no feelings," Molly said, irritated at her brother and wiping a tear from her eye.

Mama closed the radio and sniffled. "Molly has good news," she said.

Joey looked at Molly.

"I made the RA," she said.

Joey made a bugle of his hand. "Tah-rah!" he said, blowing into it. "A star is born. Congratulations."

"Thanks," Molly said, feeling shy suddenly.

"The way she's going, she'll soon catch up to me," Joey said to Mama.

"Naaah," Molly said, denying the possibility but pleased at her brother's words. "Don't forget arithmetic," she added.

Joey made Molly feel like a star all afternoon. Mama did too. Every neighbor who came in heard the news. Joey blew into his fist and announced the news to Papa and Aunt Bessie when they came home from work.

"That's enough," Molly said when Mama told the neighbors in the courtyard as she hung out wash.

"Why?" Mama said. "We don't make a force out of you every day."

Molly smiled. "Fuss, Ma, not force," she said, correcting her mother.

After supper Molly and her family went into the living room to listen to the radio. Jack Benny and Mary Livingston were on, then Walter Winchell. Speaking over the rat-tat-tat sound of a ticker tape, he gave the news:

Good evening, Mr. and Mrs. America, and all ships at sea. Six weeks ago the Jews of the Warsaw Ghetto revolted against their German slave masters.

The Jews fought a brave fight and held the powerful German army off for a long time. The battle is now over. The Ratzis—I mean Nazis—won. The Jews who remained alive after the fighting were sent to concentration camps.

Molly could not bring herself to look up and see the faces of her parents and aunt. Walter Winchell's voice droned on, but everyone had stopped listening. Mama, Papa, and Aunt Bessie went into the kitchen. Molly knew they were going in there to drink tea and feel sad.

The children stayed in the living room.

"It's your day, Molly," Joey said. "What do you want to hear next? You get to choose. *The Lone Ranger*?"

"I don't care," Molly said.

"What about you, Rebecca?" Joey asked.

Rebecca shrugged.

"What do you want to hear, Yaaki?" Joey asked.

"A song," Yaaki said. "Sing a song."

That seemed like a good idea to Molly. "Why don't you, Joey?" she said. "It might make them feel better. Let's go be with them," she added, nodding toward the kitchen.

Joey shut the radio, and Molly and her brothers and sister joined Mama, Papa, and Aunt Bessie in the kitchen. They sat around the table. The soft sounds of neighbors' voices could be heard in the courtyard.

"I'll play," Yaaki said, lifting his comb wrapped with toilet paper to his lips.

"Not now, Yaaki," Molly said. "Maybe Joey will sing for us," she added, as if it were a fresh idea.

Joey needed no coaxing tonight. "I'll sing 'Besame Mucho,' " he said and began.

12 *Eli*

In the auditorium, the graduation rehearsal was underway. Molly marched down the aisle with her class listening to the music teacher play "Land of Hope and Glory" on the piano and Miss Smith call, "Right! Right!" telling the class what foot to come down on so everyone marched together.

"Fine!" the principal said when the rehearsal was over. "Only try to look a little happier for the real thing. Some of you look like you swallowed worms."

Molly clasped a hand over her mouth, recalling the fig cookies, and turned to look at Tsippi, who made a face back and nodded.

"The photographer is in the school yard," the principal said. "He has set up a little area on which you'll stand. You'll see it—chairs for the first row and platforms behind. Each class will be photographed separately. So line up with your class."

Molly and Tsippi broke away from the others in the

aisle to get their autograph books from the seats where they had left them, then went out into the school yard. They went up to Miss Smith, who was watching the photographer seat the first class for a picture.

Molly felt a tug at her heart as she looked at the teacher. In the excitement of graduation, Molly had almost forgotten how much she loved Miss Smith. She had an urge to confess that she had cheated in the beginning, now that it was all over.

"I want the teacher's autograph," she said, going up to Miss Smith.

"Miss Smith," she said, unable to say more. The words stuck in her throat. "Would you write something in my book?" she asked, handing the teacher her autograph book. She read what Miss Smith had written: "I enjoyed your poem about Mayor La Guardia, and clean hands. Keep writing. Affectionately, Edna Smith."

Molly felt puzzled and confused. Was Miss Smith talking about the poem, or about the test?

"It was a good poem," Miss Smith said, mussing Molly's hair.

Molly felt a wave of love for the teacher. "I will never, ever cheat again," she said to herself. "I'll never have a better teacher than you, Miss Smith," she said, hurrying away before she began to cry.

"Miss Smith!" the photographer called.

"This way, class," she said, leading the way.

"Take your same places as in class, kids," the photographer said. "First row in the first row, etc."

As Molly glanced at the chairs in the first row, she remembered Miss Smith's words about pictures being forever. She did not want to see herself seated next to Beverly for the rest of her life. She waited for Beverly to sit down, then sat two seats away. Molly pretended not to understand the complaint of the girl whose seat she had taken.

"Sit anywhere!" Miss Smith said, bringing order.

"That looks fine," the photographer said, looking into the camera. "Don't move around, there in back! Now, when I count to three, smile." He turned a dial on the camera. "One-two-smile!" he said.

Molly tried to smile but her face felt frozen.

"Next!" the photographer called, asking for the next group.

Molly and Tsippi got their autograph books from the ground where they had left them, and went to sit on the ledge to wait for their friends. The other girls were also getting their pictures taken. They had arranged to meet when they were all through. Soon they came running, waving their autograph books.

"*Oy!*" Little Naomi said. "I dread seeing what I look like."

"Me too," Big Naomi said. "My eyes closed when he snapped."

"Mine too," Lila said.

Julie came running over, blowing her hair out of her

eyes. She thrust her autograph book at Little Naomi.

"I have everybody's autograph but yours and Lily's," she said.

"I don't have yours either," Little Naomi said, handing her own book to Julie.

The girls wrote in each other's books, then read aloud what the others had written.

Little Naomi read: "She's silent and bound to shine, a perfect lady all the time."

Lila then read what Julie had written: "Don't make love in a cornfield—corns have ears."

Molly laughed with the others.

Julie then read what Little Naomi and Lily had written: "May your success be as long as Mr. Jordan's nose." And, "As o'er the world you go, a friend will become a foe, but you'll never find a friend like your dear mother."

"You're the second person who wrote that in my book," Julie said to Lily.

Molly was surprised to look up and see Eli standing there.

"You're the only girl in our class whose autograph I don't have," he said, handing over his book.

Molly felt flustered. Eli had never spoken so directly to her before. "You don't have any either," she said. She laughed at her mistake and corrected herself. "I mean, I don't have your autograph either," she said, giving her book to him.

Molly stared at the blank page. Something she had

seen written in someone else's book came to her mind: "My heart pants for you," with a drawing of a pair of pants substituted for the word. But she didn't know him well enough to say that. So she wrote instead, "Good luck in all you do."

"Thanks," Eli said, reading. He returned Molly's book and walked off.

"Gee, he's handsome," Little Naomi said, watching him walk away.

"What'd he write?" Tsippi asked.

"I don't know," Molly said, holding the book.

"Read it," Big Naomi said.

Molly opened the book and read, "I write these simple words to thee. When you see them, think of me."

"Wow, he must like you," Tsippi said. "All he wrote in mine was, 'Good luck.' "

"A lot of kids write that," Molly said, trying to make what he had written seem less important.

"No one wrote it in my book," Julie said.

"Mine either," Lila said.

The girls sat awhile longer, talking, exchanging autographs with others who passed, then got up to go home, agreeing to meet again later in the day at Molly's house and go for a walk on Thirteenth Avenue.

Molly walked home alone, dreamily fingering the smooth cover of the autograph book, thinking of the words Eli had written. She had hoped to sit down quietly at home by herself and read for a while but the house was crowded with people. Mama sat at the kitchen table, sipping tea with some women. Joey was in his room, listening to the baseball game with the door closed. Molly could hear the announcer's voice through the door. She went into the living room where Yaaki was playing his comb and Rebecca was practicing the poem she had to recite for school.

"Molly," Rebecca said, "would you listen to me and see if I know it?"

Molly didn't especially want to, but she put her books down and said, "Go ahead."

"I'm supposed to recite with feeling," Rebecca said. Molly nodded.

Yaaki stopped playing to listen as Rebecca began.

> *"I had a little pony,*
> *his name was Apple Gray,*
> *I lent him to a lady*
> *to ride a mile away.*
>
> *"She whipped him [whipping motion],*
> *she slashed him [slashing motion],*
> *she rode him through the mire [wiping her*
> * shoes on the floor].*
> *I would not lend my pony now*
> *for all the lady's hire."*

"I don't think the horse's name is right. Check it," Molly said, hurrying away.

"But was it good?" Rebecca called after her.

112

"Very good," Molly said, passing through the kitchen on her way out.

Mama looked at her. "You came in, and you didn't even notice," she said.

"Notice what?" Molly asked.

"You still don't notice," Mama said with a grin, nodding toward a sheet of paper that was propped up on a glass before her.

The women around the table were smiling. "You have to congratulate your mother," one of them said.

"I got promoted too," Mama said.

Molly went up to the sheet and looked at it. "Certificate of Naturalization," she said, reading aloud.

"My citizenship paper!" Mama said, beaming. "It came this morning."

Molly felt warm and happy all over. "Ma, I'm so proud of you. Congratulations," she said, hugging Mama and giving her a kiss.

"Now, when President Roosevelt says, 'My fellow Americans,' he'll mean me too," Mama said.

The door opened and a neighbor entered. "I heard your citizenship paper came," she said to Mama. "*Mazel tov*, congratulations!"

Molly left the commotion in the kitchen, opened the front door, and went out. She sat down on the stoop, stretching her legs out in front of herself, and leaned back to think about the words Eli had written. To her amazement, in the same moment that she thought about Eli, she saw him. He was on the other side of the street, carrying a suit and looking about. He saw her and crossed over.

Molly quickly took her legs down and sat correctly.

"Hi," he said.

"Hi," she answered.

"I knew you lived in one of these houses, but I didn't know which one."

"This one," Molly said, pointing.

He nodded, looking at the house. "I was going to ask you in school, but you're always with your friends," he said. "Tommy Dorsey is at the Roxy, and the movie is *Jane Eyre*, with Orson Welles."

Molly nodded, and swallowed the lump in her throat.

"I saved up to take a date," Eli continued. "And I was wondering if you would like to come with me. For graduation?"

Molly felt dizzy. Was he asking her for a date? The Roxy was in Manhattan. She had never been there. She had never been out of Brooklyn. She wondered if she had heard right.

"I love *Jane Eyre*," she said, hoping he would repeat the invitation, so she could be sure.

"Does that mean you'll go?" he asked.

"I have to ask my mother," she said. "But she'll probably say yes," she added quickly, not wanting to discourage him.

"Great," he said and started to go. "Can you give me your answer in school tomorrow?" he asked, turning back.

Molly nodded. She could run inside and let him know in a second. But she didn't want to seem too anxious.

"So you'll let me know?"

Molly nodded again, wishing he would leave so she could breathe.

"Well, now I know where you live," he said, glancing at the house.

"Uh-huh," Molly said, looking at the building and nodding.

He took the harmonica from his back pocket. "It keeps me company," he said, and began to play "Anniversary Waltz" as he walked away. Molly watched him go for a moment, then ran inside.

"Ma," she called, standing near the door. "Can I see you for a second?"

Mama, sitting at the table with her friends and talking, looked up.

"It's private," Molly said.

Mama got up. "This is a picture of my sister. She's two years younger than me," she said, handing a snapshot to one of the women and leaving the table.

"There's a boy in my class," Molly whispered to her mother.

Mama nodded.

"He's the smartest boy in the class."

"Yes, so?"

"He's a hard worker and has a job already."

"What kind of job?"

"He delivers for the tailor."

"I see—"

"He's a musician too. He plays the harmonica."

"This is what you wanted to tell me in private?" Mama asked.

Molly came to the point. "Ma," she said. "He asked me to go to the movies with him—for graduation. All the girls have dates."

"What's his name?" Mama asked.

Molly knew Mama was trying to find out if he was Jewish.

"Eli," she said. "Tikochinsky," she added with a smile.

Mama grinned. She turned to the women at the table. "Molly has a date!" she called.

The women turned and smiled.

"Ma!" Molly said.

Rebecca and Yaaki came in from the living room.

"Where is it?" Rebecca said, looking at Molly's hand.

"Not that kind of date," Mama said, laughing. "She has a date with a boy—for graduation."

Joey's door opened. "Molly has a date!" he sang as he danced up to the refrigerator, took a soda, and danced back to his room.

Yaaki made loud noises on his comb.

Molly stood for a moment as if in a trance.

Mama went back to the table. "—I left a large family in Poland," Molly heard her mother say. "Who knows how they are. Even if they are—"

Rebecca went up to the women at the table.

"Do you want to hear me recite?" she asked.

Molly turned and walked out the door. Once more she seated herself on the stoop, legs stretched out in front of herself. She was not ready to experience the happiness she felt. Not yet. She wanted to hold it off a moment longer. She watched the street as if she had no other thought in mind.

The Good Humor man drove up to the curb and tinkled his bell. Children came running from everywhere. The street was yellow and warm and full of happy sounds. Molly thought how different it looked in winter, when the hot-knish man rolled his tin wagon down an empty, cold street and a few tough boys cooked potatoes over the fire in the empty lot.

She couldn't hold her happy thoughts back. She had made the RA! Mama had become a citizen! Eli had asked her out! Surely God had rewarded her for not cheating. A shadow crossed her happiness. Hitler was still there, in Europe, killing Jews. And what of Mama's family in Poland? Molly sighed. Maybe God was helping them too. Maybe they were all right. She hoped so. "Please," she said to God.

Happiness came rolling over her like a giant wave. She could almost see Eli standing there, near the bottom step, in his white shirt and knickers, his hair, the dimple in his chin. How could she not have noticed him before? In her mind's eye she watched him take the harmonica out of his pocket and walk away playing. The sound was sweet and made her heart melt.

Her happiness song burst out. It always did, whenever she felt great joy. Shouting the words behind closed lips, but saying them under her breath, so no one else could hear, she sang,

> "I should worry, I should care,
> I should marry a millionaire."